Almost
Havana

Almost Havana

F.W. Belland

Chris Belland

**The New
Atlantian Library**

THE NEW ATLANTIAN LIBRARY
is an imprint of
ABSOLUTELY AMAZING eBOOKS

Published by Whiz Bang LLC, 926 Truman Avenue, Key West, Florida 33040, USA.

For information contact:
Publisher@AbsolutelyAmazingEbooks.com
ISBN-13: 978-0692378885 (New Atlantian Library, The)
ISBN-10: 069237888X

Almost
Havana

Dedicated to our mother,
Jean Belland Douthit
and our wives,
Carmen and Piper

PART ONE

Short Stories by
F. W. Belland

ALMOST HAVANA

I don't know much but, brother, I know about where I've lived my whole life: Key West. Except for when the army sent me away I'd never been any farther north than Miami.

Someone used to carry me almost to Havana, though. That's how he liked to put it: Almost Havana. That one was old Willie Russell.

Cap'n Willie was a line fisherman, snapper and yellow tail, all at night when it's best and he taught me about tides and moons and baits ... but mostly he told me about Havana.

"Before that sonofabitch communist took over, Havana was the greatest place in the world," he'd say. "A city of gold." We'd be drifting over the reef on toward sundown and Willie would drink long-neck beers from the ice box and tell me these things; me just a kid dropped out of school and ready to listen to it all.

"I used to go over early as Prohibition with my father. It was fine. And after, with the big hotels and good charters, it was better. Havana is gold, boy. I'll bet it still is and we can't even go there now." He'd drink his beer and think a bit and I knew he was fixing to tell me about his bolito prize. "You see this here boat?" He'd slap the gunwale of the boat with his calloused hand all covered with liver spots and scars. "I hit the Havana bolito, El Gordo, in '53 for almost five thousand bucks. Bet a ten spot on six numbers and came out when five grand was really worth five grand! I had this boat special made just

1

how I wanted. Solid Cuban pine over Brazil mahogany ribs. They don't make boats like this no more. Make'em out of plastic." And he'd spit in the water. "This is a real boat." Old Willie'd told me the story a million times but I didn't mind. It always amused the heck out of me.

We'd idle into the edge of the reef off the rocks, the tide coming in to us and drop the rusty grapnel. I'd cut and salt the baits then put the chum bags overboard. All the while the sun was just a wink on the horizon. Willie liked to drink and would have another long neck and stare off south still thinking of Havana. "It sure was some kind of place, all right."

While it was still light and clear you could see all the way to the bottom into the rocks and fans. I diced up glass minnows and put them over the side watching them drift down and out toward where the reef came up. Then the fish came, timid at first, then pecking at the glass minnows crazy with hunger.

"We'd work like hell for half the night roping in fish and slamming them into the de-hooking slot so they fell into the icebox. It was hard work but fun. We wore strips of bicycle inner tubes on our fingers against the eighty-pound test line lest it cut us to the bone.

But when the tide slacked, changed and backed off the fish were gone in a heartbeat. Then we'd sit on the engine box and have a coffee from the thermos Cap'n Willie's old woman always stowed aboard for us. Because there was no more fishing to do, Willie would put rum in his coffee. And when he did, oft as not, he'd start in again about Havana.

"Lookit. Look over south. We drive five hours more and we could be there. Shoo, you can see the lights from the Malecon if you look hard enough."

Once I said: "Aw. Can't not. We're seventy miles from Cuba even out here, Cap'n Willie." Old Willie looked long and hard at me as if I were some little puppy.

"Boy, you got no imagination. You never been to Havana. How can you ever know?" Then he laughed and had a little more rum. "Almost Havana. Oh, child. Almost just ain't good enough."

It wasn't too much after this that the army took me. They sent me to Fort Jackson, South Carolina, then to the war. I wasn't there three months when I got my knee about completely shot off. It wasn't as bad as it sounds. Others came out worse. Or not at all. Me, I got a little pension and a good job with the Post Office. I got to go home.

I used to see old Cap'n Willie fairly regular downtown. We'd have a Cuban coffee together some mornings if he wasn't fishing. I could tell he felt bad that I was crippled and couldn't line fish with a leg like a piece of broken wood. In truth I was pretty content working at the Post Office. Fishing is a hard way to make a living, brother. Never doubt that.

I married a nice girl and we had two kids. She was from an old Key West Cuban family, catholic, but sometime into the marriage she became an Evangelical. I went along with it although I didn't much care one way or the other; I just wanted to keep the peace in our little family and it was all right that way.

It was just about that time the Mariel boatlift began, I think, in 1980 or so. I saw Willie running toward the docks one morning all crazy eyed and out of breath.

"They opened up Cuba, son," he told me. "I'm gassed

up and going." He looked at my gimpy leg not meaning to. "You can come along if you want." He was being polite.

"I got my work at the P.O., Cap'n Willie," I said. "But thanks." We shook hands. "Good luck. Maybe you'll win at bolito again."

As I could gather later, old Willie only made two trips – just to a pier and not even in Havana. Soldiers pushed folks aboard the boat and told him to get the hell away. To make things even worse the Customs and Immigration people impounded his boat when he came back to the basin in Key West. It seems that just about all the boats that hauled Cubans across got impounded. That meant they were taken out of the water and set up on chocks atop old fifty gallon fuel drums in a boat yard until the courts could decide if they'd done wrong.

I suppose you'd call Cap'n Willie an unlucky man except for when he won the bolito prize in Havana. His wife took sick with cancer and that cost him his savings before she died, bless her. All the while his boat sat drying in the sun, the Cuban pine planking going brittle as chicken bones and coming undone under their own weight, settling and warping on the chocks. The oakum fell out of the seams leaving gaps you could slide a twenty-five cent piece through.

In two years the court gave Willie back the title to the boat but nothing much was left. The engine had seized up and bums had stolen everything off her they could. One of the fuel drums had rusted through and dropped, cracking the keel and separating the transom on one side. I went with Willie to salvage what was left. He took one look at her and just walked off, leaving her there in Steadman's boat yard. He never even took the faded red "CONFISCATION" notice off the splintered windscreen.

It drained the life out of him and made him older than he was and, by then, he was old anyway. Social Security moved him to the County Home, which wasn't too bad. I visited him on Sundays and brought him cigarettes and sometimes half a pint of rum. He was always pleased to see me and talk about fishing and, of course, he never forgot Havana. We'd sit on a bench in the yard and he'd drink rum out of the bottle in the bag I'd brought.

"Well I almost made it," he'd say. "I almost got back to see it again."

Time passed. One day my wife told me we were invited on a church mission to Cuba to bring medicine to the poor. I had plenty of time off, as I was quite senior at the Post Office by now. I went out to the Home and told Willie about the trip. He was in a wheelchair now, his old veiny, bunched-up hands looked like buzzard talons on the armrests. His eyes were milky and scaled but flashed up like a gasoline fire when I told him.

"There," he said with satisfaction. "Now you'll see what I told you about. Hee hee. You go and have a look. And boy?"

"Sir?"

"Put ten bucks on the bolito for me. If it comes in we'll split it."

The airport was nice and we got put up in a hotel right on the beach. My wife was busy all day with the church folks so I had nothing to do but walk around the city. It was quite different than the hotel on the beach. Like I told you at the beginning of this story, I don't know much but I know decay when I see it. Havana made me think of old Willie's Cuban pine fishing boat: beautiful and shining and golden years ago, then dried out, broken backed and ruined in the end.

The folks were all decent enough and I spoke enough Cuban Spanish to make them smile but everything around was dusty and wanting. The buildings tottered and the old cars were held together with wire and tape.

I asked a taxi driver where I could put ten dollars on the bolito and he rolled his eyes and waggled his finger while looking at me in the cracked rear view mirror.

"Es prohibido, Señor. No existe."

So that's what I came away with from Havana.

I waited a few days to visit old Cap'n Willie, I suppose because I was afraid. Then I made up my mind to tell him the truth. I figured he had a right to know.

He sat in his wheelchair smoking the fat Cohiba I'd smuggled in and sipping at the Cuban rum I'd put in a plastic water bottle to fool Customs. Willie sipped away and exhaled the sweet cigar smoke. Finally he swiveled around in his chair and said: "So. You saw it."

"Yes sir."

A great smile came over his old toothless, wrinkled face. His eyes pin-wheeled the way they had the day of Mariel.

"A city of gold," he murmured. My resolution died.

"A city of gold," I repeated.

"Dammit, boy. I told you so."

"Yes sir."

And then he wheeled himself to face south, the smoke of the Cohiba covering his head like a cloud. I got up and said good-bye. I didn't think he heard me. Then I said: "Sorry the bolita didn't come in for us Cap'n Willie."

Willie Russell turned his head on that scrawny old neck like a rusty nut on a threaded rod. The cigar stuck out of his face at a jaunty angle. He appeared perfectly happy.

"Next time, son. It'll come in next time sure as I breathe."

THE VISITOR

Three weeks after Pearl Harbor all the people on the island left. McAllister watched them go with contempt. They were scared of the Germans. McCallister had been in the first war and Germans didn't scare him. Nothing scared him. He could handle himself good enough and besides, he reasoned, what kraut would risk coming to an island eight miles off the Florida coast to slit the throat of a worn out fisherman?

His wife was scared too, but she was more scared of him than of the Germans. McCallister disliked people and only tolerated the old woman because she'd learned to keep her trap shut. Now with everybody gone, she was lonely. McCallister watched as she fidgeted each day, moving around like a little mouse, staring in the direction of the mainland which lay under the western horizon. She wanted badly to go off like the others but was too scared to even ask.

McCallister let her hang like this for a while and then became highly amused at the look on her face when he told her: "Whyn't you take the supply boat to Miami and stay with your Ma for a while? It'd be safer." The old woman couldn't light out fast enough what with being afraid McCallister would change his mind and make her stay.

And so he was left alone. A man from the government came out once on the supply boat and left him a wireless radio transmitter so he could report anything 'unusual'. McCallister said he would and then stashed the wireless under the bed. He didn't even want that to bother him. Being alone was best.

If you asked him, McCallister probably couldn't tell you when he'd begun enjoying solitude. It was probably from spending so much time on the boat fishing by himself. People annoyed him with their yammering. Even interesting people became an annoyance after a time.

Months passed. The supply boat came with less and less frequency. The boat crew changed (probably all drafted into the army McCallister figured) and a sour Cuban who barely spoke English and his boy saw to running things. McCallister didn't mind. Sometimes he took his bundle of mail and canned goods with barely a nod of his head at the Cubans. He could have done without them entirely because there was plenty to eat on the island and McCallister had shelves of staples and magazines and dime western novels. Half a year into the war the supply boat stopped coming. McCallister felt a disconnected new sense of freedom.

The island was not large, but it offered a variety of things to do. McCallister fished from a small skiff in the mangroves or waded in the shallows to bully net lobster. From the ruins of an old citrus plantation he cultivated yams, and such trees as suited his needs, while the jungle overran the rest. In the afternoons, when the sun was low, he walked the beach to see what the ocean had cast up. The Gulf Stream ran very close to the island, you could see its deep blue not more than a mile out, and all manner of things came ashore.

Ship convoys to and from the Panama Canal passed and McCallister watched them with binoculars. Rough seas would knock things from their decks and McCallister recovered them. When the German submarines began sinking the ships, flotsam littered the beach. The submarines did not attack in the day because airplanes and fat, sausage-shaped dirigibles came out from the mainland to watch over the convoys. But at night McCallister would watch the burning hulks float lazily northward on the current until they either went down or faded from sight. Bunker oil coated the rocks and sand of the shore waiting for the high tides to wash it away.

McCallister wondered what sort of men were on the ships. He had this thought all at once one day after he'd been alone for a year: It would be a diversion to see someone. He didn't miss company, he told himself, but it would be a diversion to see a person. Even the sour old Cuban. It would amuse him. That night he hooked up the antenna for the wireless set the government man left him, but the batteries were dead and rats had gnawed the insulation off the main cables. Well, he thought, it doesn't matter. Being here alone is better.

Still, time passed differently for McCallister, more slowly somehow. His dollar watch had quit working and he drove a stake in the sand of the beach in front of the house so he could follow the shadow of the sun. The shadow moved painfully and McCallister paid attention to where it lay several times during each day. He awoke in the night and could not get back to sleep. I don't exercise enough, he said to himself. I need to work harder at something.

During the next week McCallister took his machete and cleared the lianas away from more citrus trees on the old planting grounds. The fruit would be wasted but the

labor gave him some satisfaction. When he'd finished
though, a small hollowness began wheedling inside his
being and he struggled to think what he might do next.

The season changed. It became cooler and the first of
the northeasterlies began blowing, roughing the near
water to an iron gray. The ship convoys came in endless
lines. McCallister had never seen the like, so many ships at
once. And at night the unfortunate ones burned brightly,
the tankers bursting like roman candles. Seeing them that
way turned McCallister's flesh all prickly as though he'd
been rubbed with ice. For long hours into the evening he
would sit on the porch listening to the palm leaves rustle
against the tin roof of the house and watching the burning.
McCallister did not recognize it as such, but a feeling of
sympathy for the men on the ships touched him. "Them
poor sons of a bitches," he said to the dark. One morning a
bloated corpse came ashore, bursting its buttons,
stenching, gelatinous and covered with flies. McCallister
turned away and did not come back to that part of the
beach until the tide carried the thing off.

On a Sunday, after McCallister had taken his nap, he
went down the steps of the cottage and stood on the beach.
The landscape was littered with every kind of junk
imaginable; cork life vests, cans, planks, bottles, oars, fuel
drums, spars and truck tires scattered themselves among
the oily stones of the shore. There was so much junk that
the man simply ignored it, staring instead out at the ocean.
Oddly, there were no ships today. No smudges of smoke
beneath the horizon. It was as if the sea had made up her
mind to cleanse herself after so much turmoil. Still,

McCallister searched and he finally saw something. It floated, quite far out, angular and dark against the steely water.

The wind was more east of north and the norther stalled what he saw against the current of the Stream. Very slowly it drifted toward where McCallister stood in front of his house. The man knew it would take many hours for the thing to come and so he went on with his work. He was distracted . Close to nightfall he looked through the binoculars. It was a raft of some kind, the object, rather high out of the water. Beyond that, he couldn't tell. Even though he knew it was probably nothing worthwhile, a queer expectation rose within him. In the last light McCallister ate his supper on the porch so he could watch and try to guess where the raft would come to land.

The wind picked up during the night. A shutter came loose jarring McCallister awake with its banging. After he secured it he could not go back to sleep. He thought about the raft. From the position of the constellations he knew morning could not be far off. He made some coffee and settled into a chair on the porch thinking how close to the beach the raft could be. The fronds rustled against the house and combers rumbled in with monotony. When McCallister opened his eyes again it was fully daylight and it made him jump as if in a fright.

Without washing, McCallister hurried downs the steps to the shore. He could see the raft a hundred yards to the south, beached by the receding tide. He walked briskly to it, studying its construction as he approached. It was high because someone had lashed three empty fuel drums together and tied a hatch grating atop them. Whoever built it had had some time. Something lay on the grating. Even before McCallister got all the way there he knew it was a man or what had been a man.

The body was not like the first one. This one had been at sea for a long time; McCallister could tell by the bird droppings and weed growing on the bottom of the raft. The corpse had done its bloating and unbloating and since it was out of the water, the combination of sun, wind, salt and fuel oil had mummified it like something you'd see in National Geographic. The eyes, of course, were gone, and the leather skin was black as any Cap Haitian stevedore McCallister'd ever known. Out of the desiccated mouth, fine teeth, square as dominoes, made into an affable grin. A stiff shock of blond hair fanned out electrically from the skull. Some sort of uniform, blown to tatters, clung to the skeletal frame. There was barely an odor at all, no more than what came from a box of salted cod. McCallister took a stick and tapped the arched rib cage and the sunk-down abdomen.

"God damn, boy," McCallister said. "Looks like you been missing out on your rations lately. Haw! Haw! Haw!"

McCallister laughed so hard he finally had to hold his sides and sit down in the sand and wipe the tears out of the corners of his eyes. That he was speaking aloud to a dead man did not occur as odd to him. The very act of speaking at all, of hearing his voice, gave him an enormous sense of joy.

The ebbing wavelets of the going-out tide still buoyed the raft and gently rocked it, which made the dead man's head appear to nod encouragement at McCallister's humor. God knows, McCallister thought, the poor bastard never'll get tired of his grinning.

"Come on, old son," McCallister told him. "Let's take you a little closer to the house." He laid hold of a length of rope which trailed the raft, pushed against the drum with his back and, when the little vessel was re-launched, he dragged her through the shallows then beached her directly in front of his cottage.

It was hard work, hot, as the sun had come fully up. McCallister went to the kitchen and, from the old kerosene refrigerator he got a jelly glass full of cold water and returned to the raft. The corpse still grinned and nodded.

"I don't suppose a drink of this'd do you much good now, boy. Ohh, Haw!" McCallister doubled over and almost had to sit down again in his mirth. The other kept on grinning and McCallister noted that, what with the dried up skin crusted in white salt, it wasn't such a bad thing to see.

McCallister decided to surf fish that day to be near the raft. He was excited and didn't know why. He got his pole and, from a pen in the rocks, some live crawfish to use for bait. While he worked over the gear he loudly explained to the corpse what he was doing and why. When he wasn't talking he whistled and sang songs he hadn't sung since he was a child.

The fishing was good. A school of mackerel moved through and McCallister hauled in half a dozen. He let four go. The old kerosene reefer wouldn't hold them and even a fool could catch a fish.

"Hell, Fritzie. I put a pole in your hand, you'd catch as good as me." McCallister had invented a name, figuring his guest for a kraut because of the blond hair and the uniform. Who could tell? McCallister didn't much care but the fiction amused him like nothing else had for a long time. "Shoo," he told him. "You don't look so scary, Fritz. You ain't even hardly a growed up man."

McCallister got hungry. For his lunch he made a sandwich of tinned life boat biscuit and cheese he'd salvaged. He sat on the porch in the shade where he could keep an eye on the raft. During his nap in the hottest part of the day, McCallister got up twice to see that it was still there. When he rose, he had a glass of rum.

The ball of sun lowered itself. McCallister walked down to the raft and built a fire pit to cook the mackerel. He built it near the raft so as to be close enough to talk.

"This here's the best way for mackerel, Fritzie. But you want to let the fire go to coals and put a little lard on the fish so they don't go dry. Mackerel don't taste for beans when it goes dry."

McCallister wasn't big on drinking, but tonight he kept sipping at the rum bottle as he prepared his meal. It made him light in the head, drinking, and he wondered why he didn't do it more often. He buried some yams in the cinders at the edge of the fire and set a can of peas close to warm. While he worked he told Fritz about the island and how he'd gone off to the war in '17 and all about the fishing he'd done since. In the saying of the things - the words - McCallister's mind opened up to what he hadn't thought of in years. He tipped the rum bottle back and put the mackerel on the grill.

The meal tasted the best McCallister could recall. Even better than when the old woman cooked for him or when he ate in restaurants up in Miami. He finished and had more rum then piled driftwood on the cook fire. It blazed wonderfully and McCallister could see old Fritz grinning on his raft.

McCallister walked up to the house and got his harmonica. When he returned he piled more wood on the fire and threw an old canvas lug sail over a mount of dry seaweed to make a soft place to recline and smoke a cigarette. He took some more rum and played tunes from his youth. Sometimes he sang the words between fits of playing. The songs left him a little melancholy but not in a terrible way, just kind of happy and sad and warm inside.

The fire died. The moon rose and gave a good light. McCallister saw a shooting star. He was tired and a contentedness settled on his being. In a little while he got up and pissed then walked over to Fritz. The moonlight made the boy look all right there. Happy. McCallister took the blanket he'd draped over his own shoulders and spread it on the body, tucking it right up to the chin. He returned to the sail cloth after that and lay down, curling up like a cat. It was a splendid night, cool, and the breeze came like a blessing off the sea.

In the morning the raft was gone, carried off by the high tide. McCallister pushed up on his elbows to look seaward and swore a little at himself for not tethering it. But it was all right. It wouldn't drift far against the northeaster. He'd walk the beach and find it, he reckoned. Even if he had to rig a sail on the skiff and go to the next island over the channel, he'd find the raft. His head hurt from rum drinking. McCallister lay back and watched the new sun. It was all right. He'd find the raft and bring the boy home.

A GOOD PAIR OF SHOES

On the sand beach, right before the shale cliff crumbled into the sea, a rusted trawler had been cast up. She lay there broken, immovable, part of the landscape, booms collapsed making fingers which buried themselves into the dirt.

Charles Eliot walked under the shadow of the bow, stepping carefully over the volcanic black sand and into the place where the shale banks had fallen. It was hot on the beach. He looked up the cliff wondering about it, about the way the horizontal shale had been thrown up by the convulsions of the earth. He had a drink from his canteen, a heavy aluminum thing covered in cloth. In a moment he continued his march, rubber shower shoes making squelching sounds until the sun dried them. When they're dry, he thought, it'll be easier climbing over the rocks.

It was not tough going. The shale slabs were broad and roughened by the weather. It was like climbing over awkward flights of stairs: first up, then down and always the water of the Pacific Ocean bashing nicely close by your feet. Charlie thought it was quite pleasant, the rocks and the sea and the sun burning in the sky. He looked at the government surplus compass hooked to his watch band. The needle swung south of west toward the border of Costa Rica. Charlie always wore the compass when traveling, even if his wife made fun of him. In truth, he needed the compass more to find his way in strange city streets rather than in the bush. He could find his way in the bush. During the war he'd learned to survive there, compass or no.

Charlie thought about the war. It had ruined a lot of men. Others, the lucky ones like himself (or unlucky as it turned out), had been awarded a momentary sense of true worth and purpose. In four years he'd gelled and hardened to an exquisite diamond brilliance only to fall cruelly like a spent rocket fluttering impotently to earth. Everything before and after the event became a quiet process of dissolution and irrelevancy: cheap corporate murder, wives and infidelities, luxury purchased on thin credit. Things, really. Half feelings. But never that brilliance again. Not ever. Early on he was dazed at the loss. Bemusement turned to fear. Where had the grandness gone? A tired emptiness filled his soul. Charles once considered blowing his brains out or driving a car over the lip of the Grand Canyon – he'd known a man who'd done it – quite dramatic, that. In the end, logic or cowardice or lethargy prevailed. Charles took a long breath and waited. A continuance unfolded itself before him, harmless and acceptable. Barely. Now, so many years later, he'd quit it, the useless inward questioning. He contented himself in mostly not caring too much anymore. Not about war or himself or anything, safe in the knowledge that one day he would simply die – he hoped not too painfully. At times it became almost laughable. Indeed, Charles often laughed at himself.

"Ha, ha. We are in a cell."

Charlie's head snapped up at the voice. It came

tentatively, almost embarrassed, in English. In a coved-out niche in the shale wall two men crouched. The speaker grinned. Half his teeth were missing. The second man was hard to see in the dimness.

"You're not in a cell," Charlie told the man. "You are in a cave. There's a difference." He spoke slowly as if to an idiot. The speaker shrugged, denying the distinction between cave and cell.

"It is only a manner of speaking, Señor."

Both men rose off their haunches and Charlie watched them scrabble down the loose rock, partly sliding on their back sides to be on the same level as the hard slab where he stood by the water. Charlie was irritated at the interruption of his solitude.

"I am Jesus." The speaker of English wiped a dusty hand on ragged shorts and extended it to Charlie Eliot. Charlie took it, not to be rude. The hand was weak and limp as a child's. "He," the man nodded over his shoulder, "is a friend." The other stood away and looked toward a flock of gulls. Both men were small, dark mestizos, dressed in raggedy shorts and tee shirts and thin rubber sandals like Eliot's. The friend carried a worn set of swim goggles and short wooden lobster gaff with an 8/o hook lashed to its tip. For a moment Eliot had the crazy idea they might try to rob him. He wasn't afraid. He was big as both of them and could lay his hand on a rock quickly enough. Besides, he mused, I left my wallet in the hotel.

"My friend and I are searching for lobster but it's too muddy here." Eliot looked at the turbulent water and back at the mestizo. "We were going to sell the lobster so that I might buy a pair of shoes."

"You have shoes," Eliot told him.

"No. I need better shoes. I am crossing the border tonight through the jungle." Jesus squinted up at Charles. "A good pair of shoes."

"Why cross the border? Where are your papers?" Jesus shrugged again, a gesture of patience at the necessity of not answering directly. He said, "I'm from the other coast. A Mosquito Indian. That is why I speak English. If I get to San Jose, I can perhaps become a guide, but I need shoes. Do you think I speak well?"

"Passable," Charles Eliot told him. Jesus waited a moment more, a long moment as if he expected something to happen.

"Well," he said. "We will go look for lobsters." He turned in the direction of his friend.

"Wait," Charles said. Jesus turned around. "Take this." He slipped the compass off his wrist and handed it to the man. Jesus' eyes became momentarily wider before contracting. "It might help you. And this." He gave him the canteen. "Sell it and buy some shoes. I have no money to give you."

"Gracias, Señor." Jesus backed slowly away as if Charles might change his mind. "You are quite kind." Charles inclined his head dismissively, wondering if he'd been taken. He was an easy touch. He always gave money to any bum who asked him.

"Buena suerte," Charles told him. He began walking.

"Señor." Charles Eliot turned and looked back at the brown man holding the compass and canteen he'd once owned. "When you go home to the United States, please tell the National Geographic Magazine to write about the

Mosquitos. Tell them to send someone to take our pictures. We are an interesting people."

"I'll see what I can do," Charles told him. Jesus raised his hand with solemnity then the two mestizos walked shoulder to shoulder over the shale, Jesus' chance at life was much improved now. Charles Eliot envied him. With a compass and a good pair of shoes the possibilities were endless.

SIXTEEN PUPPIES

Everyone said you couldn't remember these things but Buddy Elliot did. He never lost consciousness. He heard the first rocket coming, making a sound like bacon sizzling in a skillet and he ran for the bunker. But it got him. If you heard it, it was always too late. That's what everyone said.

Corporal Jefferson, blood splattered all over his shirt, held Buddy's good hand and stroked his forehead to keep him quiet until the medevac chopper set down, its rotors whop-whop-whopping, throwing up dust and trash like a storm. They flew him out of the fire base, rising rapidly and peeling off toward the South China Sea. Buddy was strapped tight against the vibrating metal floor, shock and cold making his teeth chatter. He had the thought: I'm going to die. But he did not.

In Danang the docs put a bandage on his head and trimmed off what was left of the fourth and fifth fingers of his right hand. At the hospital in Okinawa he waited about a month before the bandage came off his head. It wasn't as awful as he'd imagined. Part of his ear was gone and he couldn't hear out of it. He figured he could let his hair grow to cover the ear. It was all right, he guessed. The docs said the hearing might come back but Buddy developed a habit of turning his good ear to anyone who had anything to say to him. No one said much but he turned to hear anyway. The army sent him home and Buddy was glad.

Buddy had saved some money. Also, his mother gave

him five thousand dollars which had been left to him when his father had died while he was in the hospital. Buddy stayed around the house for a while and then went back to his college up state beyond the Georgia flatlands where the country had some contour. He did not know what else to do. He'd liked school before the army and thought it would be good to go back. All his old class mates were gone, of course. The new students seemed very young and regarded him with suspicion. Buddy tried to be like them. He walked around campus with the bad hand stuck in his pocket like a dirty secret. But he didn't fool anyone. Sometimes he wanted to say out loud: "Look at me. Look at me. I'm just like you." But he didn't. That would be crazy.

One day Buddy sat beside a girl in class. He ached for her as if he had broken glass in his chest. She was pretty and wore a blue pin which said "LOVE" on her blouse. When he settled into the chair, the girl got to her feet and picked up her books. Her face pinched itself with an anger, mouth red-distorted. She told him: "You'll get everything you deserve for everything you did." Then she moved to a place on the other side of the room. For many weeks Buddy was puzzled over what she thought he'd done. The girl wouldn't ever look at him and after a while the ache he'd felt for her went away.

With some of his money he bought an old farmhouse in the country pretty far away from folks. School was easy. The GI Bill and the disability check made for plenty of jack – more than he needed – and he was all right. Every afternoon when classes let out he bought a bottle of vodka and drank it on the way to his little house. He liked the man at the liquor store. The man had had his foot blown off on D-Day and it sort of made a bond between them. The liquor store man said: "Whyn't you come over to the VFW some night, kid?" Buddy said, "Maybe", but didn't and the liquor store man, Ken was his name, didn't push him about it. Ken was someone to talk to, though. Buddy liked him. Ken gave him all the free ice he wanted.

At night Buddy read and drank and sat bedside the wood burning stove. The rest of the little house was cold but Buddy did not mind. He liked being alone drinking beside the fire. He would open the fire box door and watch the coals go from white to red to black making nice pictures in his mind, then he would stir them, put on more wood and begin all over again.

One night a cat came to the porch. Buddy fed the cat. The cat came again and again and Buddy fed it and when it got quite cold the cat came inside and sat with Buddy beside the stove. From then on the cat lived with Buddy.

Buddy had a decent car and went out some. He met a girl at a carnival. He won her a pair of goldfish by knocking down ten pins with a soft ball but when he thought the girl would come home with him she gave him the goldfish and left with someone else.

Buddy put the fish in a bowl and next morning bought an aerator because he knew the fish would die if they couldn't breathe. He greatly wanted them to live. Later he got them a bigger tank with colored gravel on the bottom and a ceramic arch to swim under. The fish were quite happy swimming round and round.

Buddy had stolen a lot of things from the army. He did not think of it as stealing; he'd just taken things he'd come across and because the company clerk was his friend, he'd been able to crate the stuff up and send it home without inspection. Buddy had a Chinese assault rifle, a watch with a luminous dial, and a jungle-green cargo chute which he draped over his narrow bed in the loft of the farmhouse. He also had a standard issue entrenching shovel which folded into itself and fitted into a canvas pouch, and a .45 caliber pistol he'd lifted from the holster of a dead American captain. Buddy always thought the pistol would give him an edge, that he would use it, and now (he could not tell you why) at night when he drank vodka, and read and sat beside the fire with the cat, he kept the .45 loaded and tucked in his waistband like he used to in the war.

One night a van pulled off the road into his drive, lights bouncing up and down, one dimmer than its twin, and stopped in front of the house. The van was ancient, ruinous. A man dismounted and behind him jumped the shadow of a dog.

"Elliot. Elliot! That you up there? Don't shoot me, boy." Elliot recognized the voice at once. Then in the smoldering headlights appeared his friend, the old company clerk, Corporal Jefferson. He was black and large boned, yet now somehow he seemed shrunken. The dog hung to his heels. "It's me. Jefferson."

Buddy came down the porch stairs and stared at Jefferson. He looked bad. The skin had fallen off his bones.

"You okay, Jeff?" To himself, Buddy's voice sounded foreign. Jefferson only stared at him and then put his arms around Buddy and held him close. Jeff smelled of sweat and fear, still Buddy was glad of his touch. When he'd held

Buddy that way for a while he pushed back.

"They cut me loose, old son. I'm civilian Jeff now." Their faces were close. "You're a hard man to find."

"What happened after I left?"

The negro looked at him, eyes shot with red. "It didn't get no better, man." He shook his head. "Never. I don't think about it any more. I'm going west. I'm going to California. California's a good place to go."

"Come into the house, Jeff," Buddy told him. Buddy lead the way and Jefferson followed, dog at his side, and they sat before the stove. He made Jeff a vodka drink. The dog didn't move, not even when the cat walked past.

The dog was nice to look at, medium in build, very black and shiny, an inquisitive, intelligent look on her face. Jefferson drank what Buddy gave him. "That dog's blacker than I am," he said and laughed the way he used to, big white teeth sparkling. But in the light of the fire Buddy could see the grey pouches, finely wrinkled, which lay beneath his eyes.

They drank a good deal and said little. Jefferson tried to be jolly. "Things going to change for me, Buddy. Things going to get better." The dog looked up at both of them. Buddy gave her a bowl of water. It grew late. "G'on and sack out, Buddy," Jefferson told him. "I got me a sleeping bag."

Buddy climbed the ladder to his loft and got under the green parachute and covers and went to sleep, laying the pistol beneath the mattress of the bed. Some time in the night he rose and urinated off the balcony into the yard. Before he returned to bed he looked down from the loft. Jefferson still sat beside the dying stove, dog by his side.

29

He'd tied a rubber tube around his biceps and Buddy watched as he raised a vein in his arm and injected himself with the contents of a syringe. Buddy felt a little drunk and sick so he went back to his nest under the green nylon parachute. He looked into the darkness for a while, then placed an arm across his face and prayed for the morning.

Morning came: Jefferson and the van were gone. All that was left was an empty glass vial and some bloody cotton balls in the trash can. And the dog. The dog sat on the porch looking at the driveway where the van had been parked. Both of them were sad at the desertion. Buddy understood but the dog didn't. He stroked the dog's ears. "Looks like Jeff's gone, old girl. I guess you're my dog now if you want." The dog regarded him with deep eyes. Her tail thumped a few times on the wooden porch. Buddy sat down beside her on the steps and ran his hand over her flanks, pausing as he touched her belly. Part of the reason Old Girl was big was because she was pregnant.

"I got a dog, Ken," Buddy told the liquor store man. "She's going to have pups." Ken cleaned the counter with a rag.

"Dogs can see to themselves pretty good, I reckon."

"I suppose. But I don't know what to do with the pups when they come."

"If she's a good dog, you can find homes for the pups. Except for the females. Put the females down quick before she has time to miss their scent. Country folk don't want females. Too expensive to fix 'em."

"She's a good dog," Buddy told him. "But I don't want to put any puppies down. It seems like a mean thing to do." Ken quit cleaning the counter. He was a patient man with a slow manner of speech.

"Well, you sort of got to, kid. You don't, they just keep making more puppies and then you're really in a mess. You see what I mean?" Ken limped to the ice box and got Buddy a can of beer. "On the house, kid," he told him.

When Buddy came home each day, Old Girl was there waiting. In the late afternoon Buddy and Old Girl walked down to the swamp behind the house. Old Girl always walked in front, sniffing the ground, looking from side to side. One day she stopped cold, dead still, hair bristling off her thick neck. She growled, stepping back slowly, pushing into Buddy's legs, pressing him away. On the path, beneath a fern, coiled a cotton mouth thick as Buddy's arm. Buddy took the .45 from his belt, drew back the hammer and fired. The snake, headless, came apart like a spring and writhed on the damp earth of the pathway. If I'd stepped on that thing, it'd probably killed me, Buddy thought.

Old Girl swelled up more and Buddy talked to Ken about her every day. Ken knew a lot about dogs. Buddy took Old Girl to the liquor store and Ken felt her stomach. "She's sure plenty swolled up, kid. She'll have more than she can feed. I can feel them. They'll starve without milk. You got to put the females down, son.

Buddy did not want to do it, but he guessed Ken was right. It was the best thing to do, he guessed. He made up a low cardboard box bed with a blanket, and put it behind the stove and he waited. He did not have to wait long. In the middle of the next week he came home to the house. Inside, Old Girl lay on her side in the box with as many pups at her tits as she could take. The rest were scattered as if someone had thrown them around the room, blind, whimpering little things, black and tan. Buddy counted sixteen of them. Old Girl looked bewildered and at once Buddy considered that she'd never had a litter before. Buddy didn't want to, but he went to get the entrenching tool.

Even though it was early spring, the ground was hard and unforgiving. The sharp blade of the shovel furrowed long slices of red clay, tough as fruit rind. The sky domed grey and Buddy could not guess at where the sun lay. He folded the tool and put it down beside the little pit he'd dug.

Inside the cabin Buddy sexed the pups, placing the males to nurse in the box with Old Girl and putting the others in another box. There were eight females and eight males; half and half. Buddy covered the females with a towel. He wondered if he ought to let Old Girl see them, then remembered what Ken told him. He took the box outside.

Buddy placed the box beside the pit. He took out the first pup. It was warm and squirmy in his hand. Buddy closed his eyes and with the flat of the entrenching shovel he knocked it on the back of the head, just hard enough so it quit moving. It did not breathe any more but still felt warm in Buddy's hand. He lay the body in the red clay and then did another one, trying to think of something else. The folded-over shovel made a metallic clunk when it hit the pup's head. Buddy told himself he was doing right, the only thing he could do, like Ken said, but he felt awfully sick and terrible. He wanted there to be another way but reckoned there wasn't. When it was over he covered the little things with the towel and filled in the hole. He packed the earth down hard.

In the house Old girl lay on her side letting the puppies suckle on her. She raised her head when Buddy came in and her eyes followed him. He patted her head, stirred the fire in the stove and made himself a large vodka drink. He felt pretty damned low but he guessed it was how things had to be sometimes.

Ken put up a sign in the liquor store advertising Old Girl's puppies. As they were weaned, farmers would come by in their pick ups, sometimes with a few serious-faced children or a weathered-out woman. The farmers looked at Old Girl then sized up the pups, hefting them, balancing them in calloused hands, finally saying: "I'll take this'n if you've a mind to give'm up." In a while the pups were all gone. Old girl seemed to have aged and grown tired. She would still raise her head when Buddy came into the room, but she wore a look of bemusement, cocking her head to the side as if to hear something which was not there. One afternoon Buddy found her scratching at the spot where he'd buried the dead pups and he told her to go away. He put a piece of plywood over the paw marks and weighted it with a cinder block. Old Girl lay on the porch and watched him. She did not go on walks with Buddy any more unless he made her.

The school term ended and Buddy decided not to go back. Not for now. His head hurt and he had trouble sleeping. The doctor at the V.A. clinic gave him some pills and when Buddy drank vodka and took the pills he would pass out on the floor. Once he fell down the porch stairs and split his chin open. If he did not take the pills he would stay up all night. A restlessness seized hold of him like a vise. One weekend he went to the nearest city and spent the night with a whore. It was not very satisfactory. The whore was scared at the sight of his hand. "Jesus Christ," she'd said. "What'd you do to your hand?" Buddy told her. She gingerly touched it with a pink index finger. "Jesus Christ. That's really somethin'."

Most nights, Buddy walked alone in the fields around the old farm house. He always carried the gun even if there was nothing to be afraid of. He would leave the lights on in the house and look at it from across the meadow. It appeared strange and theatrical. In the daytime Buddy managed to sleep some until the thrumming of helicopter rotors woke him with a sweating, skin-prickling start. But there was nothing in the sky except ragged black crows savaging the newly plowed earth. Buddy would stare long and hard at the sky then across the heat-distorted fields to the edge of the tree line. Shadowy forms flickered and disappeared in the periphery of his vision. Buddy waited for things to become different, better, but they would not.

Summer came. Just the same, Buddy liked to keep a small fire in the stove so as to sit and watch it in the night. The old tranquility he'd first had in watching the coals failed him now. Ugly visions danced in the flame.

An unease touched the small family. The cat, always aloof, refused to enter the room. Old Girl chose a corner in which to lie, away from Buddy's side. If he turned to her, the eyes showed uncomprehending sadness. Only the two fish swam about the aerator without concern for the sins of the world and would rise happily to the surface of their tank to eat what he gave them.

Buddy asked Ken: "Would you take care of Old girl if anything happened to me, Ken?"

"What's to happen to you, kid?"

"I don't know. Would you?"

"Whyn't you have a beer and relax?"

"Would you?" Ken made his face in an odd pacifying manner.

"If you say, kid. Now have a beer and relax. On the house. Christ. You're nervous as a rat."

"I feel better now," Buddy told him.

The night sky spread itself in a brilliance over the growing fields. The little house looked like a toy in the distance. Buddy had left the door open. He could see the iron stove. Buddy thought about the girl in his class who was angry. He thought of Ken and Jefferson and the girl at the carnival and of the whore. He thought about the dog and her puppies and of the cat. He wished he could speak to them all at once and tell them how he was a good person, had tried to be as good as he was able, how he'd never wanted wrong. Buddy wished he could fix up every wrong ever committed anywhere and he knew that was impossible. Sometimes, he knew, things got broken so badly that nothing could fix them. It was a terrible, terrible thing.

The dead captain's pistol made a warm reassuring weight where it rested in his good hand. Ken would take the dog. The cat was clever and could look after himself. That left the goldfish, the only truly helpless and innocent creatures within the hemisphere of Buddy Elliot's view. If there was a god, Buddy hoped He would see to the care of the world but failing that, at least keep the aerator going until some kind person took pity on the two fish where they swam in happy ignorance round and round in their bowl.

THE FISH KILL

Bing waited on the boat. Hope filled his soul the way wind fills the sail on a Key West mullet skiff. Slow and shimmery in the beginning, the hope crept into his heart and ballooned it out so he thought it might burst. It'd knocked Bing flat when the magistrate gave Papadad ninety days in the stockade for being drunk, but that was then and as time drew on the hope for his father rustled and became alive so now he could barely keep it all in.

Maybe the ninety days were best for Papadad, the boy thought. When he came out, came home, he looked good. His face was firm and healthy and he walked all springy and energetic the way Bing liked.

Because he was small for a nine year old, Bing climbed up on the engine box so he could see Papadad walking toward the dock from across the dirt parking lot. Papadad walked from the Bluelights Café and carried a paper sack. Bing guessed Papadad had bought a bottle of whisky for their fishing trip but that was all right. Bing knew his great hope would carry them. They would get to fishing good on the reef and Papadad would be too busy to drink much whisky.

A little whisky was okay, Bing decided. And his hope was such that he felt he could will the old man to drink just a little. And maybe some beers too, for Bing had found a case of longnecks under the thick blanket of shaved ice in the fish box.

Galilee tipped with Papadad's weight as the old man

stepped from the dock to the gunwale and down into the cockpit. Papadad named the boat *Galilee* when he'd been Bible reading and a member of the Pentecostals. He quit the Pentecostals but kept the name painted on the stern and Bing liked it fine. It had a good sound and Bing thought if it came from the Bible it was a lucky name.

"We ready, boy?" Papadad stood outside the line of shadow cut by the cabin roof. He looked big and grand in the sunlight. His cap was on straight and he'd creased the bill like a ballplayer. Bing could have hugged him, but said, "We're ready."

Papadad stooped when he came out of the sun and into the overhang. Bing felt proud that his old man was so big.

"Let's get her started, son."

Bing helped Papadad pull back the heavy cover to the engine well. They squatted over the four cylinder Grey. The Grey was old and ugly, crouched on its mountings in the bilge. Papadad didn't like the engine. He called it a hard starter and Bing was scared to death of the big iron fly wheel with its sharp teeth. That fly wheel could flat tear your arm off. Papadad opened the fuel line and Bing watched honey colored gasoline fill the glass fuel ball. The old man cleaned the distributor cap with a rag and wasn't scared of anything.

Papadad inserted the handle into the flywheel and strained to pull it around. He grinned up at Bing, his beefy face big and happy. He winked.

"You want to spin it, son?" Bing loved it when Papadad kidded. Papadad was a great kidder.

"I ain't man enough yet, Papadad. You know that."

"Well, someday you'll be man enough. You will, won't you?"

"Yes, Papadad. Some day."

The veins knotted up in Papadad's great arms. He gave the wheel a tremendous wrench, once, twice; the engine coughed, caught, banged and caught again. It roared until Papadad eased back on the choke. Blue smoke wafted over them and Papadad kept grinning at his son. Together they replaced the cover and the Grey made a pleasant humming under their feet.

"Cast off, boy."

It was cool on the water. Cold even. Darned cold, Bing thought. But he didn't mind it. Papadad idled out to the middle of the channel. Bing watched how the chilly wind ruffled at the bits of hair which stood out from under Papadad's cap, and how, in the winter sun he could see the beard stubble defined over his cheek. Without speaking, Papadad fished out two jackets from the gear locker and handed one to Bing. Bing dove into its warmth and faced the sun just like Papadad. It was wonderful.

"Boy," Papadad said. "Fetch me one of them longnecks from under the ice. And the opener." Bing pushed himself off the side of the boat where he'd been leaning.

"All right," he told his father.

The great stone ledge near the reef lay a few miles out and to the west. Bing could see the Gulf Stream running hard blue beyond. The ball of sun had an hour's time left above the horizon when Papadad loosed the grapnel. He shut down the engine.

Bing and his father rigged the hand lines. The cold got worse and with the sun going down it got worse still.

Galilee rested bow to the wind, tide trailing off the stern. In the last of the sunlight Bing stared hard into the surface of the water. Forty feet down he saw the schools of mangrove snapper. He tossed a handful of salted glass minnows overboard. The water eddied around them, clear, and you could see the silver bits of glass minnow spiral down. Bing and Papadad watched the fish rise to the bait, then almost as if they had one mind they shied away and settled back in a lethargy. Papadad stood silent then said:

"I'll be damned. Never seen them turn away from glass minnows." He scratched under his cap tipping the rim forward. "Maybe it's the cold. Never seen it get this cold south of Miami. And hell it's cold." He drained off his beer. "Fetch the lantern, Bing."

Papadad fired the lantern and he and Bing cast their lines over. The sun went. Again the fish rose in a cloud, turned and fell back toward the bottom without taking the baits. In the cold light of the lantern, Papadad stared into the water and drank at another beer. He screwed his face up and kept staring even when it became too dark to see the fish. They both put on rubber slickers over their jackets against the night. The cold came still and sharp like metal and Bing felt it creep into the holes of his jacket sleeves and up the flesh of his arms. Papadad brooded and finally went forward for his whisky.

"I never seen the like, boy. I wish we had us a thermometer." He drank from the whisky bottle, then the beer bottle, and shuddered when he swallowed. "I'll bet it's close to freezing. Almost." He drank again. Astern the trailing lines dripped daggers of phosphorescence among the bits of chum. No fish rose. The water stretched flat under the icy stars. The clarity of the sky made Bing shiver. Papadad put his arm around the boy. The rubber of their slickers made a creaky sound and Bing smelled the sweet whisky on Papadad's breath where it came warm on his cheek. "Best you go forward, boy. Cuddle yourself up in the bunk for a spell."

"I better stay with you, Papadad. What if the fish start biting?" The old man laughed, not unkindly.

"Go do like I say, Bing. I'll come for you if there's fish."

Bing did as he was told. He felt he ought to stay up with Papadad, fish or no. But the closeness of the cabin felt good. He crawled into the bunk and pulled a salty smelling army blanket over himself. Maybe he would call out to Papadad once in a while so he wouldn't be alone with the whisky. In his warmth Bing caused himself to not think of whisky drinking and thought instead of a yacht all varnished and bright and the thought became a dream - he and Papadad owned the yacht and piloted themselves all the way to England or maybe China like in a book. It would be grand. Then for a long time Bing dreamed nothing.

"Bing. Bing!" The boat was turned. They were off the stone ledge. Bing could feel it.

"We're off the ledge," he said to the darkness.

"I know." Papadad was breathless, excited. "I slipped the anchor when I saw what I saw. We're drifting landward." He wavered unsteadily in the gloom of the cabin. The gas lantern had gone out and the sliver of moon was well up. It looked close to daybreak. "For god sake, come on, boy."

Papadad peeled back the blanket. The cold struck

Bing, colder than anything he'd felt in his life. Papadad pulled him from the bunk by the arm.

"Boy, this is something. It's a miracle I only seen once." Papadad kept pulling him until they were on deck. Papadad could hardly stand and held himself up on the gunwale. "Look!" he cried hoarsely. He waved his arm at the low mangrove islands where they'd drifted. Over the sea lay more than false dawn. In the queer light Bing saw patches on the water. Not patches, fish, hundreds of fish floating on the top of the flat calm. Thousands. He shivered. They were surrounded by fish, white bellies to the sky, thick to the point of bumping into one another, bumping against the hull of the boat. "It's a fish kill, boy. The cold's stunned them near dead." Bing stared at the fish then at Papadad. Bing figured he must have gotten a new whisky bottle because he drank from a full quart. He capped the bottle and wiped his mouth on his hand. "It's a goddamned miracle. Just like Jesus and the disciples in the Sea of *Galilee*." He shook Bing by the shoulder. "Don't you see? All we got to do is dip them up. We'll be rich, son." Papadad's eyes cartwheeled like two bloodied eggs. "Get the bully nets. Hurry."

Bing stumbled forward and found the long handled nets. Papadad wandered from side to side looking at the fish and muttering to himself. The boy returned to his father thinking how they were lucky and would be rich, but a foreboding darted at the numbed cap of his brain.

Bing and Papadad began dipping up the fish. Papadad worked like an engine but the whisky made him clumsy. He hauled up fish three and four at a time, slinging them toward the ice box. In a fit of impatience Papadad took off the hatch top and balanced it on the gunwale while he shoveled fish in. He lurched toward the side and knocked the hatch top hard. It teetered and fell into the water with a splash. Bing tried to reach it with the handle of his net. It slipped away.

"Leave it, boy. Leave it." The old man panted like a dog. "Leave the goddamned thing. We'll make another. Just get them fish into the box." Bing watched the hatch cover drift slowly from them then began dipping up fish again as Papadad told him.

Some of the fish were truly dead, others moved their fins and gills in convulsions. The fishbox filled rapidly. What little shaved ice remained was overwhelmed and disappeared beneath the slithering, gasping fish. Papadad didn't slow down. He began making a pile in the stern of the boat. The sun came up in a rush and the scaled fish hides glistened wetly in the light.

"What about ice, Papadad?"

"Don't need ice, boy. S'cold enough." The old man would not even look at him now. He kept his head down where the bullynet was, wildly slinging more fish aboard, tottering from side to side and breathing in gasps. "Get the good ones, boy, the expensive ones." He'd lost his ball cap and perspiration glued curls of hair to his face. "Get the big ones!"

Bing closed his ears to the awful noise Papadad made and studied hard on the fish. They were heavy and his arms ached. He tried for the best ones, the pretty ones the market would use for display and pay the most for. The fish stared back at him from where he'd stacked them into a pile. Bing felt sorry for them then, but he kept working.

He worked hard and the work warmed him. Only his fingers were still numbed from the cold of the sea. In an hour he'd taken off his jacket. The sun was hot on the back of his neck. He looked up suddenly and saw that all was quiet and that he was alone. Papadad's net lay on the deck.

"Papadad!" He screamed. The old man had gone over the side he just knew it. "Papadad!" Bing ran forward looking into the water. "Oh. Papadad." Half blinded in his tears Bing turned and turned trying to see everywhere at once out toward the horizon. Then at the door of the cabin he almost tripped over the soles of his father's boots. The boots hung off the bunk. "Papadad." Bing knelt on the deck beside the bunk and shook him. The big head lolled as if the man's neck had been broken. A thread of saliva bled from the corner of the mouth and eye whites showed from slitted lids. "We have to get the fish in, Papadad. They'll spoil if we don't take them in now. Papadad. Get up. Please." Papadad breathed long and deep and as Bing shook him all the harder, the man began to snore.

Bing left his father and returned to the cockpit stepping around the piles of dead fish. The sun had gotten good and warm, now. With all his strength Bing raised the cover of the engine well, straining himself until little fuzzy specks danced before his eyes. The old Grey hunched in its place like an oily beast. Bing opened the fuel line and inserted the handle into the great iron fly wheel. He switched the ignition toggle then braced and pulled with both hands. The fly wheel moved a quarter of an inch and would move no more.

Bing sat down, his feet dangling in the bilge. The thought came that he ought to try again. He didn't. It would be no use. "It's all so unfair," he told himself. He didn't deserve it. Then he knew fairness had nothing to do with anything, that this was how things were for him and Papadad, how things always were and that he couldn't change it. Before he realized he was doing it, Bing began planning how he would manage. He'd have to take care of the old man for a couple of days now until he got over being sick from the whisky. He could do that. He figured he'd better get the five dollars out of the tobacco can and hide it for later. There were things he needed to do, things he'd done before.

Bing rested on the lip of the engine well and looked at the teeth on the Grey's flywheel. He wondered then why he'd ever been afraid of it before. It wasn't much at all, really. Just an old rusty piece of iron. An average man could turn it. Even a small man or a big kid. He hated the Grey. If *Galilee* was his boat, he'd rip it out and throw it over the side. That would be the first thing he'd do if he could, and he'd do it right then even if they had to row home. The idea almost made him laugh out loud. He couldn't wait to tell it to Papadad. Papadad was a great kidder, wasn't he?

Bing felt the cold evaporate. On deck the sun beat down from a cloudless sky and the smell of ruined fish grew as the boat drifted before a small breeze which rose from the Gulf Stream.

KILLER STEVE

There's no money in raking sponges any more so hardly anyone does it. A few Cubans do it, I suppose because they don't know anything else and can't speak English well enough to get a regular job. Maybe they just like the work. I don't know. In the evenings you can see them in their skiffs down in the shallows at the Bight. Before the city built the docks there I used to pull my truck off on the other side of the bridge and drink a few beers and watch them. They sat in the skiffs and beat the sponges with wooden paddles to break them up inside. None of them talked and all you heard was the smack-smacking of the paddles across the water. Curing a sponge is a long affair and I don't see how it can be worth much, but Cubans are persistent people.

Killer Steve wasn't persistent and he wasn't Cuban. He was the only American I knew to go for sponging because that was all he had left. He and his partner, a sour old *guajiro*, both close to bums, would pull out each morning, the *guajiro* hauling the skiff behind a broken-down, one-lung wooden boat. That's how it was. Now it's just the *guajiro*, because while I don't believe Killer Steve ever killed anyone, someone sure killed him good and dead.

John's bar is up on Division Street by the old commercial pier. Yesterday was an early day so I got off my boat and walked into John's to have a drink. John's is a small place, with a door in the front and a door in the back and a dozen tables near the bar. Fat John and Willie

Russell, the charter captain, were the only ones there.

"Well, they found your boy Killer Steve at the high tide line this morning, Buddy," John told me. It was as though he was repeating a story he'd just told Willie. I guess I was entitled to the story since Steve had worked for me on and off. "Throat cut so far back that just the bone held his head from falling clean off." Happy, he waited. "Remember the last time he was in here?" I remembered. "He was a jerk. A scrawny, big mouth, cruddy jerk." John waited again. "It had to happen, you know. I mean some time." I knew. He and Willie nodded at each other. Everyone knew.

John's is not a place I'd take my wife, but I went there for drinks by myself. The last time I saw Steve I'd come in after a good catch. I sat drinking quietly at the end of the bar, sometimes nodding at people I knew; quiet, just wanting to have my drink and relax. Steve came in.

He wasn't a bad looking boy but if you studied him, you saw a wrongness. Maybe it was drink, but he had a tight face like a cripple who is always in a small amount of pain, and that meanness that some cripples wear like a badge for being crippled for so long. He didn't see me and I was glad. At the same time I got to watch him. I watched the things he did. Let me tell you that he got his name Killer because he would get liquor courage and then become mean and liquor brave. He got beat up a lot. It was his life and I guess he never knew better.

Mostly Steve was a thief. Today he had a girl with him - a sally girl, sad, drunk - she followed him like a dog. What Steve was doing now was waiting until someone left a table or a half-empty glass and then he and his sally girl would take the rest of the drink and pocket the change.

The bar crowded itself; smoke lay thick, foggy, hiding and no one cared about Steve. He was drunk, badly drunk, staggering around drinking free. Fat John looked at him once. I saw his anger, but Fat John had paying customers to serve in a hurry. Steve robbed change and finished half-glasses of beer, towing his sally girl astern, the invisible painter secured round her thin neck as if she were a sponge skiff. I placed the cup of my palm to my face but he saw me just the same.

"Buddy." He stank. My son in the Catholic school would be his age, but I had no feeling just then. Only that he stank so badly and that his eyes were red as blood. "My girl." He pulled the sally girl over by the elbow. He wavered on the balls of his feet. The girl wouldn't look at me. I saw she could maybe be pretty. I wanted to get the hell out. I'd felt damned good before this but now all I wanted was to leave. "This here's my girl," he told me. The sally girl wiped her nose on her hand and kept refusing to look at me or anything. Steve eased onto the stool beside me and left her standing. He looked at me. His bleeding eyes were terrible. In better times I'd see them clear blue with the ocean reflecting into them. His youth, neglected as if it could never die, leaked from his face. "Lemme two bucks, willya, Cap'n Buddy?"

The sincerity came so close to me, harmless, the eyes looking even more deeply into my own, wanting to believe in themselves as much as I wanted to believe in the lie.

"No," I told him.

"Come on." It was a whine.

"You owe me five already."

Steve's head wavered while he engaged me. In the

49

belief that he was invisible in his drunkenness, he moved. I marked his thin hand reaching for the bills beside my glass. The sally girl, her eyes closed, swayed back and forth to the sound of the music which came from the box.

I am a big man and when Steve touched my money I took his wrist hard, thinking that the same wrist had pulled lines on my boat in the better times. We froze that way.

"Get away," I said. I felt him harden. "Quit it and get away from me."

He could not let it alone, his nature would not let it be. Steve plunged, twisted, became unbalanced and, stepping back, fell squarely into the table behind. Fat John jumped over the bar quick as a cat and grabbed Steve's collar. Steve strained at the man, pointing his fists at me. Howls and curses came from the patrons. One man wiped the spilled beer from his trousers and threw the wet towel into Steve's face. Steve blanched and then went all livid, knowing he'd pushed himself to that stupid point where a man must do something, anything. No one would ever hit Fat John, so I got ready to bust him when he raised his skinny fists.

"Kill him, Stevie." The sally girl lurched against Fat John. "Kill him!" Steve stood still waiting until his collar was loosed, then he turned and hit the girl with the full weight of his open hand. She fell half over to her hands and knees and when Steve made for the door, scrabbled after him like a broken crab. She cried hard, blubbering. Steve ignored her and stopped at the door. He looked back inside. He looked at me, clearly, not angry, only drunk and confused as if we'd disagreed on politics. I wished I'd given him the damned two dollars. That was the thought I had when he disappeared.

I sat down. Fat John brought me one on the house and I drank it slowly. I must have sat there half an hour or more just being quiet. The crowd thinned out and I was about to go. An ease had only just settled itself on me when the door slapped open and we could all see Steve. Fat John stiffened the way he does when he gets ready for trouble. Steve's face had changed. He might have had a high fever the way the dark parts of his eyes glistened through the red like bits of metal on a dirty floor. He made straight for me and I figured I was going to have to hit him this time. Standing there in front of me he twisted his mouth in different ways as if God had manufactured his flesh out of putty. So suddenly that it scared me, he took a roll of bills from his back pocket and grinned like an idiot.

"Cap'n Buddy," he said. "Here's the five I owe you." And he put a fiver on the bar. Then he tossed the rest of the money, I guessed about twenty bucks, toward Fat John. "And here's for drinks for the bar." Steve looked around a minute or two then went to the door and stopped. In a very conversational voice he said back to us, "You bunch of son of bitches." Then he left.

The bar quieted itself then made a lot of talk about Steve and the money; they all drank it up no matter what they felt about him. Me, I was feeling more uneasy all the time. I didn't finish the drink Steve'd bought but put on my cap and went down to the docks to where my boat was. I walked the scuffed planks, stepping over the frayed mooring lines until I got to her.

The tide was down. I got into the cockpit and sure

enough there lay the poor sally girl curled up against the gunwale, her little fist into her cheek sleeping like a child. Hell, she was a child. Her eye had begun to color where Steve'd smacked her. I left her be and looked to what I knew I'd find. The hasp on the cabin door was wrenched off, hanging by one bronze screw on the old mahogany frame. Through the hole I saw how the radio had been torn out. I looked at it for a while. It was an expensive piece of gear, a radio like that. Inside my guts I wanted myself angry, the way I thought I ought to be, but the sad busted door and the girl asleep on the deck just made me want to go home. I figured I'd find Steve soon enough and square things. But I never did.

"I figure it was the Cuban that done him," Willie said.

"Or someone he crossed. Hell, he asked for it." Fat John wiped an imaginary spill on the bar. "That dumb bastard could never quit pushing things. No one'll ever know. They can look for a hundred years and never find out who done it."

Willie Russell swirled what was in the bottom of his glass and drank it off. "Yeah," he said. "Who cares any how?"

I left them talking and went into the street. I fixed my cap to keep the sun out of my face. If I'd given up the two dollars maybe things would have been different. For a while. But Fat John was right. I figured Steve would have gotten it some time because he asked for it. Maybe he was born for it to happen. In truth and sorrow I might have drawn the blade myself.

52

THE DYING MAN

Florentino Pico did not have a high opinion of himself and he imagined (correctly) that neither did anyone else. Why should they? He was entirely bland without one accomplishment.

Florentino lived and worked in the small Caribbean port city of Deseado, a five hour train ride from the capital. Aside from making that trip once a year to visit an old aunt, he had never been anywhere in his life.

For twenty years, since his sixteenth birthday, Florentino had worked in the counting house of Don Alejando Mendez. From his small window in front of the high desk he could see the waterfront and the forest of great masts of the freight schooners. When he'd been younger the ships had enchanted him: where had they been? Where were they going? He often thought of sailing away on one of them but he was too timid. And besides, he had his mother to care for. When his mother finally died he'd long given up such fanciful thinking of travel.

Florentino owned two dark broadcloth suits, shiny with age. The best was for Sunday mass; the other for going to and from work on the trolley, which passed the room where he lived, and carried him for ten centavos to the wharves each day at seven and home at five.

He had no close friends. People tended to forget his name. Even the priest, when shaking his hand after Mass on Sundays, would usually be talking to someone else.

Florentino was racked by love for his landlady's

daughter, Sta. Celestina. He could barely stand to see her out walking with the rude, loutish boys of the town but knew that anyone as young and beautiful as she could never find interest in a man such as himself. He was ridiculous to look at: balding, round-faced as a pink moon, bespeckled and shaped like a pear.

His only passion was writing poetry which he did secretly at night in his room. He sent the poems to the literary magazines in the capital. They were never published.

In the whole of his time on earth nothing remarkable had ever happened to Florentino. And then one day he fell ill.

The illness did not come all at once but gradually, and then seemed to accelerate. The color left his cheeks. He lost weight. His face took on an ascetic character. The first one to say anything was Sta. Celestina. He met her in the foyer as he came home from work.

"Why Don Florentino. You don't appear at all well. Do take care of yourself." She had taken his hand briefly and squeezed it. Florentino was too flabbergasted to reply.

In another week Don Alejandro came to his desk. "My boy. You look ghastly." He gave him an envelope. "Here's some money. I want you to take the train into the capital and consult with a doctor friend I have there. You are one of my best workers, you know." Florentino almost fell off his stool. Don Alejandro had never complimented him once in twenty years.

That night Florentino searched his features in the glass. If he did look ghastly his appearance bore a pained dignity he found attractive.

The specialist in the capital was an Englishman. He examined Florentino at great length using strange and wonderful instruments, and studied the specimens from Florentino's body with a giant twin-barreled brass microscope. After a time he had Florentino sit down in a comfortable stuffed chair in the consulting room.

"You have a rare blood disorder, Sir. I regret that there is nothing to be done."

"Nothing?"

"Nothing. I am sorry."

When Florentino reported this to Don Alejandro, the old man looked stunned. "Nothing?"

"So he said, Sir. And he *is* English. It must be so." Florentino's knees felt weak and he was afraid. Don Alejandro seized both his shoulders in his hands.

"We'll make him the liar then, my boy. You've never had a proper vacation. Take one now. Take a month, two months. Whatever you need and devote it to rest. Your salary will be sent to your lodging." The old man's eyes were misty. "By Caesar, we'll prove him wrong. We'll show him what kind of men we are here on the coast!"

The condition became worse. Florentino's health spiraled downward. He slept days and feverishly wrote pages of poetry all night long.

After a time there came a tap on his door. It was Sta. Celestina with a covered bowl of soup.

"It's from Mother and me. We pray for you every day."

Celestina began asking him to sit with her in the parlor while her mother worked at cross-stitching. Celestina read famous poems to him. Twice when he looked at her in the subdued lamplight there were tears in her eyes. In the late afternoons she insisted he walk with her on the *Atrvesada* and placed her hand through his arm. The priest called and asked Florentino to attend Mass daily. He had Florentino, Celestina and her mother for tea on Sunday.

In the café, casual acquaintances with whom he hadn't spoken in months or years invited him for coffee or brandy. The post brought a letter from the capital's leading literary magazine: "My dearest Florentino Pico: Your work shows true genius. Send us everything you write." Florentino showed the letter to Celestina and she threw her arms around his neck and kissed him impulsively.

"I knew it," she cried. "I could tell how sensitive you were!"

Florentino felt himself wasting away and yet a strength seemed to grow within. He carried himself upright almost like a soldier. His sunken eyes burned as molten lead. He no longer looked ridiculous. I will accept this, he thought. It is the will of God.

After writing all night Florentino wandered the streets at sunrise when the shop boys were taking down their shutters and the municipal workers were sprinkling water on the park shrubs. He dragged himself to the market then, feeling weak, decided to retrace his steps home. When he turned an old Indian stood in front of him seeming to have materialized from air. The Indian looked to be from the uplands, the high sierras, for his clothing was rough and brightly colored. He wore a necklace of bone and glass beads. There was not a tooth in his head and his flesh was burnished leather incised with vast tributaries of finely knit wrinkles.

"Do you have faith?" the old man asked in broken

Spanish. The voice came from a deep well. For a moment Florentino could not speak, so intensely did the Indian look at him. Then he replied, stammering:

"Yes."

"Only God can save your soul, but give me one silver peso and I will save your life."

Florentino's hand shook and he withdrew a coin from his vest pocket. It disappeared into the brown, horny talon and from the folds of the colored cloak the Indian produced a large, old-fashioned bottle stopped with a dirty cork.

"Drink an apothecary's dram each morning. Fail and you will die."

"An when it is finished?"

"You will be cured."

And then he was gone. Florentino would have doubted he had really existed at all, that he'd only been a thing of his imagination if the wavy, green-glass bottle of liquid did not rest heavily in his hand.

Feeling dazed and light-headed Florentino went home. In his room he measured out a dram and drank. Still fully clothed he threw himself diagonally on the bed and immediately fell asleep.

Florentino awoke in bright sunshine. He felt refreshed. He washed and shaved. Color touched his cheeks. For the first time in a month he was hungry.

Returning from his meal at the *comedor* Florentino met Celestina in the hall. When she caught sight of him her lips parted and her eyes widened. The voice came with uncertainty.

"Dear Florentino. You look ... better."

Florentino ate four meals a day and slept deeply ten hours each night. In a week his coat no longer hung on his shoulders like an Indian cape; in two weeks he had trouble buttoning his vest. His face regained its cherubic pink roundness. He glowed with health. The local doctor pronounced him fit as a horse.

"You shouldn't believe what foreigners tell you. They'd be glad to see us all dead."

Florentino made his appearance at the office.

"Look, Don Alejandro. I am restored."

Don Alejandro wore the same baffled expression as Celestina.

"Yes. Yes, I see." A curious note of disappointment touched his voice. The other clerks gathered round him and mumbled shy congratulations, looking this way and that but never into his eyes before settling back to their counting desks, seeming embarrassed that they'd ever thought such a healthy fellow could have been ill in the first place.

After Mass the priest declared it a miracle, if only a small one, then turned away to chat with parishioners of more importance.

Celestina no longer brought him soup or sat in the parlor while her mother did her cross-stitch work. When Florentino inquired after her, the mother only shrugged. Twice Florentino saw her on the *Atravesada* arm in arm with a young man; she only gave a slight wave with her hand. Her beautiful eyes looked through him.

Now at the office Don Alejandro treated him quite formally and became unusually irritated at the slightest error.

"Florentino, you dolt. You may be cured but it hasn't improved your arithmetic!" he said once within the hearing of the others, some of whom smirked at Florentino's discomfort.

The editor of the literary magazine sent a letter. "Sr. Pico: What has become of your poems? You have hardly sent a line and what you did send is far below the quality I initially thought you capable of. An artist must suffer and work!"

Florentino was crushed. He had no one he could confide in except Celestina only now he rarely saw her. He took to lurking near the entrance of the house on the chance of meeting his love. When at last he did, she was in quite a hurry.

"I never see you any more, Sta. Celestina."

"Oh, Don Florentino," she addressed him in the formal manner as she would an old uncle. "Now that you are well you don't need such a poor nurse as I. And beside, I have become engaged. Didn't Mother tell you?" And she was off, leaving Florentino in the shadow of the empty doorway.

When Florentino stopped taking drams from the old bottle he could not tell; he did not recall that or any other thing about the ensuing weeks. A policeman found him wandering on a road outside of town, wasted to nothing, barely able to cobble words together.

Florentino opened his eyes. He was on the narrow iron cot in his room. The priest sat in one of the two chairs, murmuring as the beads of his rosary passed from finger to finger. Celestina was in the other, next to the bed. Don Alejandro stood wringing his hands and the mother of Celestina, drawn and diminished, hovered near the door.

59

The light of the paraffin lamp was dim and oppressive.

"You're awake. Dear boy! You're awake!" Don Alejandro's face contorted itself. "Thanks to God." Tears streamed down the lovely cheeks of Celestina. She placed her hands carefully upon Florentino's arm and laid her head on his shoulder. Florentino could feel the bed tremble from her subs.

"Oh, my darling," she wept. "My poor, poor dear."

The old priest rose.

"We must leave him to rest. God willing his strength will return again." When Florentino caught his eye he knew the priest did not believe this would happen.

Don Alejandro patted him on the damp shoulder where Celestina had wept. Celestina kissed his cheek – Florentino could smell her fresh scent . The priest made the sign of the cross above his head. Led by the mother, they all filed out. The door closed itself more quietly than a whisper. Florentino was alone.

He lay still for a time wondering where he'd been and how he'd gotten back then gave up the effort as too difficult.

Slowly he drew back the covers and crept out of the bed. He was dressed in a clean night shirt which warmed him against the chilled air. Holding the bedstead, he made his way to the cupboard in two steps for the room was painfully small. From there he withdrew the ancient bottle. Air bubbles in the shimmery surface sparkled in the lamplight. With fingers thin as pencils, he extracted the cork and raised it to his lips knowing he could drink life. He stopped. In resignation he instead poured the oily contents down the drain of the tiny sink. With an irony that Florentino was too simple to grasp and wholly lacking all art, bitterness or resentment, things alien to his soul, he told himself: No. It is better this way. How can I disappoint those who have so loved me?

A BLIND PONY

Don Eduardo Montealegre was a retired naval officer. Why he chose to live so far from the sea, high in the mountains in our little provincial capital, I couldn't imagine. Until I learned of his past.

Don Eduardo was a bitter man, not quite bent by age but showing a bitterness that came from inside where his soul and the bitterness shared a place. He stood tall and angular and walked as though leaning into a strong wind. He wore his white hair and whiskers cropped short; his face looked out over his well-made clothes like that of a starving horse, long and searching.

Don Eduardo came from an old family hardly tainted by Indian blood. Those before him had been soldiers and poets, senators and revolutionaries, holders of vast land grants today fallen into litigation, poverty and disrepair. When he was a young ensign, though, things had looked much better and a promising career lay before him.

In those days our country went to war with her neighbors each decade or so – never for too long – and men were given a chance to make a name for themselves. Don Eduardo's opportunity was a disaster. At the moment of closing with the enemy cruiser, he and the entire crew of the junior officers' mess were overcome with food poisoning. While the guns boomed on deck, Don Eduardo and his mates lay in sick bay tied up in their hammocks like trussed chickens. It was a humiliation which followed him like a cloud. Fifteen years later, warring again but in command at last, Don Eduardo's little ship jammed itself hard a-port and he steamed in left-handed circles until shell fire and an unseasonable storm drove the vessel upon the rocks. It was a miracle that he wasn't captured or drowned. Perhaps that would have been better, he often thought. At least he wouldn't be remembered as a buffoon. It was his last command and last promotion. Until he left the service he occupied a small, musty office in the archives section of the War Ministry. Even then it would have been bearable if his life before and after the major tragedies had not continually been plagued by wholly ridiculous events. Don Eduardo was his own greatest indignity. He was forever sneezing in church. A gust of wind knocked his cap off during parade. His nose ran. When being introduced to the President of the Republic, the top button of his tunic popped off like a brass cricket and splashed into a champagne flute. He hiccoughed unexpectedly and suffered shameful bouts of gas. I am a man cursed, he told himself.

Don Eduardo cloaked himself in cool reserve in the face of his adversities great and small, and as life went on he became cold, then frigid. His wife and two daughters were an irritation. He ignored them all and they drifted slowly away from him much in the same way his disabled frigate had drifted onto the rocks so many years before. He found himself alone, pensioned off and oddly happy that nothing remained to anchor him to his memories. The uplands, he reasoned, would be the best place for him – a place where no one knew him and where nothing would matter to him a jot.

A relative arranged the lease of a ramshackle hacienda

and the few dry manzanas of scrub and furze around it. An old Indian and his niece took care of him. He did not require much. He rose early and ate a spare breakfast on the veranda. From there he could look across the dun colored hills to the plain and then to where the horizon disappeared. At that juncture rose the great mountains, perpetually snow-capped and so huge that they appeared as giant clouds reaching to heaven.

The town itself was not much. It straddled a flat, rocky spine which traversed steep ravines and arroyos. Long ago it had been a mule route for passage through the mountains. Now it had the railroad. There was, of course, an ancient stone church, the station, a fair hotel, a few stores and cafes and a decent park with a fountain surrounded by old, gnarly pine trees.

After breakfast every day Don Eduardo would walk in to meet the 11 o'clock train from the capital in order to buy yesterday's newspapers. Then he had coffee in one of the taverns followed by lunch at the hotel. Occasionally he would call on the Magistrate or the Inspector of Police as a courtesy. But mostly he spent his time idling in the park with a book or drinking wine in the better café.

One day, during the summer of his fifth year there, he finished his lunch and went directly to the café. It was a thick-walled old place with a tile roof and wide Moorish arches that opened to the street. Beside the building was a yard, a garden of sorts and a ruined corral. As Don Eduardo entered the café he noticed that a horse was in the yard, standing very still with its head pointed toward the sidewalk, neck resting on the top rail of the fence.

He sat at his usual table and ordered a small bottle of

wine.

"What is that horse doing in the yard?" he asked the waiter.

"It is not a horse, *Señor*. It is a pony. A blind pony."

"Blind?"

"It cannot see, *Señor*."

"I know what blind is, you fool," Don Eduardo snapped. The Indians of the region were very taciturn and grave, almost morose. They often committed suicide. It was difficult to tell if they were being insolent or just ignorant. Don Eduardo would stand for neither. "I want to know how it got there."

" A *caritonista* from the rock pits left it in the road, *Señor*." The man seemed overwhelmed at needing to make so complicated an explanation. "It had only one eye to begin with and when it could not pull the cart any farther, the man beat it with a stick. He blinded its other eye. A mistake, no doubt, as it was a waste of a one-eyed pony. The *caritonista* abandoned it and my *patron* said to put it in the yard. Perhaps the tanner or the butcher will buy it." The waiter made a gesture with both hands indicating nothing. Small eyes like black flints stared momentarily out of his brown, impassive face, then away. Barbarians, thought Don Eduardo. Brutes.

Don Eduardo had never cared for animals. Cats avoided him. Even after five years the caretaker's dogs still barked when he came through the gate before slinking away, tuck-tailed sneers on their vulpine faces. Only horses held an attraction for him. In fact, if Don Eduardo had any passion at all it was for horses.

He'd been brought up to ride. His father was a

cavalryman and he had been placed upon a saddle before he could walk. In a family which discouraged any display of affection, little Eduardo found warmth in the stables. The great beasts were gentle and responsive to the child's combing of their coats or bringing them carrots and sugar. He had not thought of that part of his childhood for years.

Don Eduardo stood up and placed some money on the table. An odd sense of excitement had come over him.

"Tell your *patron* he is not to sell the pony to the butcher, the tanner or anyone else. Do you understand?" And then Don Eduardo walked out the arched door and over to the railing in front of the yard.

Even from a little distance one saw how pathetic the pony was. A tent of loose skin draped itself over a framework of bones. Don Eduardo could count every rib. One of the ears was broken, bent at an angle from the head. As Don Eduardo approached, the good ear pricked up and turned in his direction like an antenna.

"Hello, pony," said Don Eduardo. He expected her to bolt or at least move away, but the pony remained put. Carefully, Don Eduardo placed a hand on the side of her neck. The flesh quivered just a bit. The pony turned its head now and Don Eduardo felt himself start with revulsion. The head of the beast was tethered in a home-made halter of coarse jute. A wire nose piece circled the pony's muzzle, cutting a callused furrow in the flesh as though it had been gouged out with a knife. The left eye covered itself in dark scar tissue. The right was an open wound, hollow, red and angry. A fly buzzed in and then out. Don Eduardo whisked at it with his hand but it returned with new determination. The pony slowly rested her chin on the wooden fence rail again.

As carefully and gently as he was able, Don Eduardo removed the halter. It stuck in place where the worn flesh had scabbed over. Still, the pony permitted him to continue. He threw the terrible apparatus to the ground, stoking the animal with slow repetitive sweeps of his hand. The nose was dappled and soft and the teeth not in bad condition. This was a young pony. Her knees were knobby and as he looked, shuddered one against the other. It was then that he realized the thing was dying of hunger. The waiter stood in the arched doorway watching.

"You," Don Eduardo said in a measured voice so as not to frighten the pony. "Fetch a bucket of water then run up to the office of the veterinarian. Quickly!"

The veterinary surgeon was a young man, young enough not to be hardened by his profession. He went pale at the sight of the blind pony.

"Oh, dear," he said. "Oh, dear." Then to Don Eduardo, "Tell the boy to bring some fine oats and a little grain. Come. Help me bring her into the shade. I'm surprised the poor creature is still standing."

After the pony had eaten and taken water, the doctor gave her an injection of vitamins.

"And the eye?" asked Don Eduardo.

"Gone. We can only close up the socket to prevent infection. But tomorrow. When she is stronger. Today she must rest." The younger man took some gauze and a couple of bottles from his bag. "We'll clean her up and make a protective bandage for now."

The next day the veterinarian returned. He instructed Don Eduardo and three Indians how to hold the pony while he slit the upper and lower lids so he could sew them together with cat gut. When the knife sliced into the first lid, the pony's soft muzzle was against Don Eduardo's arm pit. He felt the animal flinch and he held her close, but that was all she did. Don Eduardo crooned quietly into her ear. For the rest of the operation she remained with her head resting against his shoulder.

The pony made a good recovery. She ate well and started to fill out. Don Eduardo made an agreement with the *patron*, a cheerful mestizo with a large, round stomach. A shelter was built and a boy put to watch over the pony in the night.

Don Eduardo was pleased. Each day he walked eagerly into town to see the progress of the pony. After lunch he sat at a table to watch her sunning herself in the yard. When he came to the fence she would always raise her head and make a low, nickering sound. Don Eduardo brought her carrots and sugar cubes in his pockets and the pony would nuzzle at the material of his coat with her soft, dappled nose, impatient to have a treat. He had the boy comb and brush her each day and not being satisfied with the job, took it over himself. There was Don Eduardo in his vest and shirt sleeves grooming the blind pony in the shade of the thatch-covered lean-to. If anyone thought it odd, they had the good sense to be quiet. As the weather became cooler he had a blanket fitted to keep the pony warm at night. The next month, when she became strong enough, he had another halter made for her out of loose canvas and smooth brass rings. The nose piece was wrapped in lamb's wool. In this manner, Don Eduardo was able to take her for walks out the back gate of the garden and along the narrow path which skirted the edge of the steep ravine. Don Eduardo kept the pony on a short lead, taking care to always place himself between her and the cliff's edge. The pony did not sense the precipice but she did seem to sense the presence of Don Eduardo just as though she could see him. Almost always she walked lightly touching him. Sometimes she gave his shoulder a gentle nudge with her soft dappled nose. Don Eduardo began to feel a kinship with her as strong as any he'd felt in his whole life. He and his pony walked two miles out and two miles back every day.

A change came over Don Eduardo. The Inspector of Police commented to the Magistrate how well the old fellow appeared. They all lunched together with other gentlemen of the town twice or three times a week. Don Eduardo enjoyed the company. Never in his life had he truly enjoyed the company of anyone.

A peace settled upon the man. He began thinking of his estranged daughters. He longed to see them again. They would have children of their own now and Don Eduardo envisioned himself leading the pony on the path by the arroyo with a child or two on its back. The pony was strong and sleek now and would adore the attention of children, he just knew. That very day he decided to write a letter to his wife and begin to make amends for the past. She was a decent woman. How could he have treated her so badly? In the evening, on his walk home, he composed the letter in his mind. In the letter he told his wife of the pony, hoping to convey the enchantment he felt. The great Andean sky domed out over his head. Stars blazed in the thin, dry air while a new idea formed itself in Don

Eduardo's brain. Why not, he asked himself, bring the pony to the hacienda? The simplicity of it almost caused him to physically reel. Why hadn't he done so before? Had he not been so close to the hacienda and the night been so late, he would have turned around and brought the blind pony home at once.

Don Eduardo was so excited he could not sleep the entire night. Only at dawn did he fall into a restless state of unconsciousness, startling himself awake with the full light of day steaming through the window.

He dressed hurriedly and had only coffee before putting on his coat and taking his stick and hat from the hall tree. He walked briskly and once laughed out loud thinking how odd it would be if he broke into a trot. The walk was not far but seemed to take longer than usual.

When Don Eduardo reached the town, he went directly to the café. He approached it from the side opposite the yard. The waiter and the *patron* were taking the shutters down. He reached the other side. The pony was not there. He turned. The two men were looking at him. Don Eduardo approached. The *patron* twisted the folds of his white apron and shifted uneasily on his feet. The Indian did not move at all. Don Eduardo mounted the steps to the porch beside the arched doorways.

"Where is the pony?"

"Ay, *Señor*. A terrible thing has happened." The *patron* twisted the apron with greater agitation. On the table lay the pony's soft canvas halter.

"Where is the pony?" whispered Don Eduardo.

"The boy. The stupid wretch of a boy left the gate unlatched. The poor pony wandered out in the night and fell into the arroyo. Its neck was broken so we just buried her there. I am sorry."

Don Eduardo collapsed into a chair. He put his face into both hands, his palms pressing against his eyeballs causing the sensation of red and green light inside his head. He wondered if that was what the pony saw in her blindness. When he could, he got to his feet. He picked up the halter and stepped off the porch. The *patron* and the waiter watched him walk slowly away, back bent, his gait grown suddenly ancient. A long while passed and neither man said anything. The *patron* studied the great mountains in the distance. The waiter studied nothing.

"Well," the *patron* finally said. "It was only a pony."

"A blind one at that," the waiter replied.

"I don't understand. Of what possible good is a blind pony to anyone?" asked the *patron*, finally taking his gaze from the far mountains and looking at the waiter. In all the years he had employed the waiter, the patron had never seen him smile. Now an odd curl, barely perceptible, lifted one side of the man's mouth.

"God knows, *Señor*," the Indian told him. "Only god knows."

TOTAL ECLIPSE

For many years my aunt was a pillar of the German Club in an industrial city (I won't say which one) in North America. She saw people come and go and took a great interest in their lives. She knew, as they say, the real truth about everyone. Here is a story she told me.

The activities of the German Club were, of course, curtailed during the second war. Everyone of German descent strove to be as American as they could, enlisting in the armed forces, working in plants and turning in their spare brass door keys for the munitions effort. But when the end came, people wanted to forgive and forget and go along with their lives. It was the American way.

Many Europeans arrived in those years, Germans as well as others, and the club membership swelled with the new arrivals. They were displaced persons, former prisoners of the allies, those escaping from the east. My aunt did her best to make all her countrymen feel welcome regardless of the past.

It was here that she first met Herr Kuhl. For some reason everyone took to calling him Fritz until after a while his real first name was forgotten.

Fritz Kuhl stood a bit taller than average but looked short for the brutish muscular broadness of his body. He was swarthy and barrel chested and had arms like tree trunks. I once saw him straighten a horseshoe with his bare hands. He had no affectations save for an old fashioned mustache which made him look all the more fierce; yet in spite of a swaggering demeanor, no one ever knew him to become truly angry.

Because Fritz Kuhl spoke German, Ukrainian, Polish and Russian, all sorts of speculation arose about his origins in the old country. Some said he had been a Nazi of the vilest sort; others claimed he'd fought with Red partisans. One man timidly asserted he had it on good authority that Herr Kuhl was a German Jew, indeed a rabbi who had renounced his faith.

Rubbish, my aunt told them all. He is what he appears to be. A man. A bit of flotsam who drifted here on a sea of tragedy. Let him be.

From Herr Kuhl himself came nothing for he spoke nary a word about the past. In fact, he spoke very little at all. In spite of his reputed skill at languages, he was taciturn as a stone. While playing the card game skat on a Saturday night, he only grunted replies at would-be conversationalists. A liter of dark beer might draw him out to make a lengthy statement such as: "The work at the factory is boring and tiresome. When I get capital, I shall go into business for myself. With capital and these," he held up his two fists, "I shall make my fortune." And then he would fold his great arms just so and smoke black Russian cigarettes and sip at his ale until his turn in the skat rotation came up.

Factory jobs were plentiful and Herr Kuhl, an excellent machinist, worked long hours of overtime. At the end of three years he came to my aunt, folded his arms as was his custom, and spoke in thick English around the black cigarette in his mouth: "I have saved money. I have plans. I need a wife. You will help me, yes? The request could have been more delicately put, but Herr Kuhl was not a delicate man; besides, my aunt permitted a great deal of latitude in what she termed her 'charges', that is, those who enlisted her aid and whose lives she enjoyed shaping.

"I shall see what I can do, Herr Kuhl." And here the man put his heels together, bowed clumsily, and murmured: "Dunke." To his way of thinking the arrangement was done.

Tante found Herr Kuhl a woman. She was a pleasant girl, Edith. What struck one almost at once about her were her hands, mannish and capable, the palms of which pointed rearward when she walked. She was large - but not fat - and carried a slope shouldered posture which made her arms appear overly long. Her skin shone radiant, almost olive as if she'd come from the Mediterranean, but Edith was indeed German, pink cheeked and gifted with square white teeth. Straight brown hair framed a plain face and heavy lashes with coarse brows accentuated liquid eyes which seemed ever wide with some perpetual question. An incipient mustache grew finely upon her lip. In short, she was no beauty, but somehow remarkable in her own way. She worked as a maid in a modest hotel and on weekends cleaned houses for wealthy Americans. She was cheerful and energetic, having something of a zeal for honest labor, and if hardship and tragedy had driven her from her home, she, like Herr Kuhl, never made mention of it.

My aunt introduced them, the two each knowing well the purpose of the meeting. It was a queer match viewed from afar: Herr Kuhl twenty-some years the senior of Edith, she being alone with no prospects. But Tante had insight and recognized that she guided a pair of individuals of indeterminate past whose life experience left little room for such silly American notions as romance. "In these times, practicality comes first," Tante would say. "A practical match is a good match."

Herr Kuhl only grumbled to Tante: "She's not much but I suppose she'll do," and did not so much as thank her for her efforts which my aunt forgave.

The couple married at the office of the municipal judge during their lunch hour with only Tante for a witness. Herr Kuhl returned to the factory before one o'clock and the new Frau Kuhl had only enough time to change into her maid's uniform before catching the bus back to her duties at the hotel.

And so it went for the first year. The only contention between the couple was at the German Club. Herr Kuhl discovered that his bride had a passion for playing skat, traditionally a man's game. The first time he caught her at it, he took her aside and muttered through his thick mustache, "I will not permit this. You are hardly more than a child. It's not right that you should play cards. You must obey me in this and in all things for your own good. I know what is best for you. Now go and drink coffee with the ladies." Edith meekly accepted the rebuke and sat with the women. But she sat where she could see the card players and surprised the other ladies by accurately predicting who would win and who would lose.

Beyond this incident there appeared no discord. Edith made a public point of obeying Fritz, but she was quite clever too. When Fritz worked his overtime shifts at the factory, Edith came to the club by herself and sat close to the skat players, watching and often whispering a bit of advice into some old man's hairy ear. For his part, Fritz mellowed somewhat in his new role of husband and occasionally allowed Edith to play a game or two because it amused him to see how handily she beat even the more experienced players. When he became bored with it he would say to her: "Now little mother, you've had your fun. Run along and drink a coffee with your sisters." And he would laugh mightily at the men, throwing his great body backwards in mirth, and pat his wife on the head as if she were a cherished spaniel. Edith relinquished her place at the table without expression and took a chair as near to the game as she dared. At this time she gave up smoking American cigarettes and took up the pungent black Russians. It was her first act of rebellion.

That winter Fritz brought home a little mutt he'd found outside the factory. It was scruffy and half starved. Edith nursed it back to health but even when the dog had regained meat on its bones it ate greedily everything placed before it as if it might never eat again. In the evenings Fritz enjoyed placing a bowl of table scraps on the floor and standing before it. When the dog moved to the right, Fritz moved left, blocking the animal from its supper. He did this until the dog was set to growling and barking with frustration which caused Fritz to chuckle and hold his sides. Finally he sighed with satisfaction at this joke and let the poor dog pass to gobble up its food.

This teasing exposed a new side of Fritz to Edith. While Fritz never mentioned her smoking black Russian cigarettes, Edith recognized her own transgression and sensed that he resented it, that he'd set himself upon some course of subtle revenge, and this was so. On the Saturday nights of their traditional attendance to the German Club, Fritz would often carry on a ritual that went like this:

"Tonight you shan't go with me, little mother. My God. Look at the weather outside. You'll catch your death of cold and I couldn't have that on my conscience, could I?" And he would pat her head fondly, tease the dog and set about arranging his clothes to go out alone. Edith would compress her lips and watch him from beneath her coarse brows, sitting bleakly by herself at the kitchen table. Fritz wandered about then whistled as he shaved in the bathroom. He would dress, carefully brushing off his overcoat and fedora, drape a scarf round his neck and just as he was about to throw the overcoat cape-like about his shoulders would say to Edith: "Oh, come along then. I won't have you looking so glum. The dog has a happier face than you. But I can't wait for more than five minutes. Hurry now!" And Edith would spring from the table, run a brush through her hair and struggle into her coat just as Fritz made for the front door. On a few occasions Fritz did in fact make her stay home, always for some good reason he'd invented. This act Edith saw as a design to maintain a tension and anxiety as to whether she could or could not go on any given Saturday night. All week long Edith would consider this and by Saturday morning a weaker woman would have been a bundle of nerves. Edith only set her strong square teeth and awaited what fate might bring.

She would always remind herself: Life isn't so bad and this is one small thing. There is much time for great change.

One evening in the following spring, Edith and Fritz came together to the German Club. Fritz drank two liters or dark beer, remarkable for him as he liked to always keep his wits sharp. He took Edith by the arm and led her to the table of my aunt. When they were invited to seat themselves Fritz said without preamble: "We have capital. We are ready for our own business. What do you think?" And here, as usual, he folded his arms and puffed on his black cigarette, waiting for Tante's reply.

"Es is gut," Tante said. "What do you propose?"

"I propose a grocery with cans of things and links of fat sausage," Fritz told her. "She," and he pointed to Edith without looking, as if to indicate a lesser being. "She. Hmmph. Well, let her tell you herself." And he held his head up with indignation.

Poor Edith was so shy, even with Tante, that she wouldn't raise her eyes.

"Go on," Fritz demanded. "Tell her."

"A bakery," she murmured.

"Bah! We shall fail. I know nothing of bakeries." Fritz had become quite florid.

"I do." Edith's voice was hardly a whisper and Tante suspected she bordered on weeping.

"Bah!"

"Let her speak, Fritz," Tante said and placed a hand on Edith's to give the girl courage. At once Edith lifted her face and Tante was startled at the fierce light of determination.

"We shall not fail. I know baking, my husband. If you

listen to me I will tell you what you need to know. In this you may trust me."

Neither Fritz nor Tante had ever heard Edith make such a firm declaration and Tante could see that Fritz was indeed shocked.

"Well ...," Fritz temporized. But Edith had seized the moment and poured forth quickly lest her resolve slip away.

"Leave everything to me. I have given my notice at the hotel. I will see to all the arrangements. It will take a month to prepare. You will not be sorry, Fritz." Her eyes bore the passion of a true believer.

And it was so. Many of the men Edith coached at the skat table were old timers in America, successful property owners, landlords, even a doctor and two lawyers. They did not forget their past and held to the German Club as a talisman. They were only too pleased to help the peasant girl who was master of their game.

In time a bewildered Fritz found himself with white flour up to his elbows and bits of dough clinging to his walrus mustache. Gleaming pots and kettles and strange machines clanked and whirred about the enameled workroom.

Edith gave her first concise direction, an order really, and in Fritz's mind an automatic trigger engaged itself with military precision in preparation to take the next command. And the next and the next. From great sacks of flour, through the machines, into the ovens and out to the cooling racks came an amazing variety of goods. Fritz stood in awe at the wonderful order and logic. That it had come about on the account of his Edith was lost to him, for

Edith was what? Simply Edith.

In the beginning business came slowly. Fritz was quick to despair, throwing up his flour-white hands and falling into a funk.

"I should never have allowed this. I should have stayed on at the factory. You will bring us to ruin with your hare-brained ideas, woman."

"Wait," Edith told him. "Wait."

The couple began work at two in the morning and by nine the products were on the shelves.

"Go home now and rest, Papa," Edith would tell Fritz. "You have done most of the heavy lifting. You need a sleep." The phlegmatic Fritz was open to suggestion and longed for his bed. When he had gone, Edith waited on customers until noon when a temporary shop girl came in. Edith then packed a variety of the finest wares – crisp dinner rolls with hard crusts and soft innards, pastries delicate as ice glaze, and elegant cakes which melted on the tongue – into a peasant's straw basket and went each day by street car to a different restaurant in the city. To the managers of these places she would curtsy in the old fashioned manner and say:

"Esteemed sir. I am Edith Kuhl of Herr Kuhl's bakery. Herr Kuhl has bidden me to prepare a small gift for you and to say that if we can be of service to your fine establishment it would be an honor."

The managers were highly amused at this peculiar young woman, some laughing outright. But when they tasted what Frau Kuhl had prepared, their laughter stopped. Edith, shy at first, became bolder, and to those managers who showed promise she returned again and again, learning their names and inquiring after their families. Always she brought something new and interesting. It was not long before Edith had hired a full time shop girl and then two. Fritz remained master of the baking room, understanding now the mechanics of the process but always dependent upon Edith for the magic of her creative gift. He gave her no praise and she expected none. Instead, she employed two young men to aid her husband in hefting the hundredweight sacks of flour for the labor was arduous and Fritz was not the man he used to be.

In two years Edith purchased the building and expanded the bakery. She flew about like a bee. She was everywhere at once from the work room where Fritz and his helpers labored, to the sparkling showcases and marble topped counters in front, to the office where she tabulated the account books. It was only in the office that she smoked her black Russian cigarettes, for she would not permit smoking, even by Fritz, in the work room or store front. To better keep in touch with her customers, Edith bought a Chevrolet motor car and learned to drive. She put on a respectable amount of weight as became a matron, cut her hair short and straightened her posture so that her dark eyes looked smartly and forcefully ahead when she joked and cajoled her clients. The black Russian cigarettes were now clamped in an ebony holder. Her accent evaporated and she wore well made blue jackets and skirts and low heeled hand-stitched shoes. Quite suddenly and quite naturally she found herself to be a very capable woman.

One night as Fritz prepared his usual joke on the dog

Edith said in English: "God dammit, Fritz. Feed the poor beast and stop tormenting him. I'm sick of this foolishness!" And she glared at her husband from over the top of the ledger. Fritz's mouth opened like a trap door then closed. He placed the bowl before the dog and stepped aside, never trifling with the animal again.

On Saturday nights Edith often got to the German Club in her Chevrolet ahead of Fritz, for Fritz had become more and more fond of sleeping. When Fritz arrived he would find his wife at the head skat table, her black Russian cigarette in its ebony holder, skillfully laying down set after set at a a penny a point while causing her fellow players to laugh over stories of growing potatoes in the lowlands south of the Rhine, what cows gave the best milk, or how a peasant could always best a city dweller in a deal.

Fritz took to having two and often four liters of dark beer on a long night. Despite his size he looked somehow diminished, pale as if the flour in which he worked had ingrained itself into his flesh. His belly sagged and his eyes, red-rimmed, drooped over bluish pouches of fat.

In the thirteenth year of the bakery, an unlucky year, Fritz had a stroke and had it not been for the quick action of his assistants, he would have surely drowned face down in a vat of gelatinous dough.

The stroke left Fritz bound to a wheelchair, the left side of his body useless and stuttering with palsy. But Edith could well see to his care, for Herr Kuhl's bakery was now the largest in the city with half a dozen outlets and all the major restaurants as clients. Further, Edith had listened to and weighed the advice of the seasoned businessmen at the skat table and made wise investments in real estate. Hence, though they still lived in a modest apartment downtown, Edith had a permanent maid to look after Fritz. She needed only to keep black Russian cigarettes away from him as the doctor declared he mustn't smoke in his condition. When she caught him sneaking one she'd snatch it from his lips and snuff it out. "It's for your own good, little father," she would say. And then Edith would go on brusquely about her business, for she still rose at two each morning to supervise the bakery and care for her clients' special needs. But always Edith made time in her day for a game or two of skat at the German Club.

Each Saturday night the maid and one of the bakery assistants would help Edith bundle Fritz and his wheelchair into the Chevrolet for a night at the German Club. But only if the weather permitted. It pained Edith to say: "Little father – look at the snow coming down. You'll catch your death." Fritz had now poor ability at speech and would grow red in the face, mumbling a protest. Edith would wipe the saliva off his chin and touch his head affectionately. "Bertha," she called to the maid. "Put Herr Kuhl in front of the television. I'm going out for a while."

Edith, in the name of Kuhl Bakery, became the prime benefactress of the German Club. On the twentieth anniversary of the opening of the first shop, the German Club held a celebration in the Kuhls' honor. Old Fritz was wheeled up to the podium and sat mutely beside Edith while Tante gave a marvelous speech extolling the virtues of the Kuhls and how they had attained the American dream.

Edith listened, her face shining. The ebony cigarette holder was an elegant extension of her hand and the smoke of the black Russian wafted across the immobile face of her husband. Tante turned to Edith with a grand gesture and Edith rose to great applause, everyone getting to their feet. She embraced Tante then stepped to the microphone, clamped the ebony holder in her brilliant square teeth and clasped her large hands together like a prize fighter.

"Life is good!" she said in German. "Ja. Life is good." And she faced Fritz, grey-faced and ill, caressing his sunken shoulders and kissing the top of his bald head. "Life is good, ja little father?"

The old man's mouth twisted, wrinkling his paper skin but no words came out. His body shivered mightily and it was impossible to tell whether it was simply an attack of palsy or if he quaked in his soul with impotent rage.

THE THIEF

Frances Elliot liked cats. He sat on a lower tier of the Coliseum ruins in early summer sunshine feeding half a dozen of the sly, suspicious creatures. Every day for more than a week he bought expensive sausage at the little market so he could feed the cats; he could afford it. Hell, he thought. I could probably feed all the cats in Rome.

Frances' wife liked cats, too. They each had one in their New York brownstone flat. When they went to the summer house or on winter vacation to the islands they always brought the cats. Frances' cat was old without many teeth. He slept away a good part of his life in a wooden bowl on top of the refrigerator. Being as the cat was almost toothless, he drooled and Frances wiped his chin with a paper towel and the old tom purred, Frances guessed, because it felt good to him to have his gums rubbed. Frances' wife said it was disgusting but she did not truly feel that way, Frances knew.

Her cat, the wife's, was a rotund tortoiseshell, sulky and lazy who loved only that woman. On cold nights the cat would curl into his wife's belly like a child. Frances and his wife had no children. They had money and two cats.

Frances rose and dusted the seat of his tailored trousers, leaving the last of the expensive meat on a paper for the Coliseum cats. He had a thought about how the old girl, the wife, was doing. Probably golfing or lunching at a club somewhere. Certainly not engaged in an affair. Not now. After thirty five years together they'd passed that part with the scenes and threats and recriminations. It had all seemed so dreadfully important at the time. Now they existed easily, almost on separate planes. They'd reached a truce, much as the old tom and the tortoiseshell. Frances wondered if in not having had children they had evolved into one another's parent, gently scolding, mutually supportive in moments of despair. Life had been quite odd in that respect and would become more so or perhaps less when he took early retirement next year. He could barely imagine it. Then he thought: nothing will change. It will go on and on and on and one day it will simply stop. Frances Elliot was not particularly saddened by this.

Plenty of time remained for his only appointment of the day so he walked up the little embankment, crossed the Via Cavour and headed north. It was a good day for walking and, despite having drunk too much the night before, Frances enjoyed the pavement beneath his feet. He walked until just before he broke a sweat – like a racehorse – then stepped aboard the Number 64 bus.

The press of people on the bus annoyed Frances but he thought, why not be a good sport? He would take a cab home. Frances held the overhead bar; there were no empty seats. By bending his neck slightly he could see the stores move by in a blur. The bus wasn't so bad. Frances thought of nothing then, only the swaying and jostling of the people near him. The contact remained anonymous, almost fraternal, when something stirred in the back of Frances' brain. A thing moved against his thigh, stealthily and with a secret, almost erotic sensitivity.

Frances awoke, eyes addressing fully the hand inching its way into his front pants pocket. Despite a dissolute life,

Frances kept fit by playing handball and swimming. He could be quick. With both his fists he grasped the slender hand which sought the few paltry lire in the pocket – change from buying food for the cats. He seized it hard and wrenched it back mightily, feeling the metacarpals crunching against one another. Only when he had the hand out and crushed did he look to its owner. A thin man, young, staggered back, released now. He'd gone white under a dark olive complexion. Two day's beard appeared as pen strokes against his taut flesh. Frances knew only a rage at the attempted violation. Logic left him. Should he throw a punch? Point and cry out a denunciation? All the while he thought, the thief sidled away as Frances, large and square shouldered, tried clumsily to pursue him moving his bulk as if mired in lard. The thief seemed to turn edgewise like a piece of paper and slip through the crowd toward the door, half looking and half voiding the glare of Frances Elliot in his wrath. The pale face showed a mixture of fear and resignation. Frances hesitated, considering, and the bus settled into the curb, pneumatic doors opening, allowing the thief to melt away like water. Frances watched him dissolve into the swirl of the sidewalk, moving furtively and seemingly low to the ground like an injured cat, beaten, tattered and dirty, holding his wounded paw to protect it from further harm. The thief looked back once and was gone. The bus pulled away and Frances collapsed into a seat. That son of a bitch, he thought. He felt for the money. It was still there. The crooked little bastard. He scowled at the rest of the passengers, all oblivious. I hope I broke his hand.

Frances rested his head against the glass, realizing he

trembled with rage. Or was it indignation? He took several deep breaths and quit. No harm done, he thought. Still … Oh, stop it. It was nothing.

Frances crossed his hands in his lap, allowing himself to be mesmerized by the fashionable shops which passed the window. And then he felt badly. The emotion birthed itself and grew in the emptiness of Frances Elliot's soul. He recognized it. The thief had been hardly more than a boy. He could have been Frances' son.

Against his will, Frances formulated what the thief's life was like: tentative as the cats in the Coliseum; how he would return to a shabby room somewhere and count his losses; how each morning he, the thief, awoke from troubled sleep with the need to simply survive. Alone. In that they were spiritually the same, he and the thief. If I'd had the boy, he would be different. It would not have taken so much to change him, to change the both of them from what they'd become. Frances Elliot fell so deeply into the thinking of his loss that he missed his stop and never realized it until the bus reached the end of the line.

PART TWO

Short Stories by

Chris Belland

THE REMEMBERING TREE

The unexpected rap on the door startled Emily Pinder enough that she spilled a little coffee from her cup into the saucer. Not a lot, just enough to fill the indentation at the bottom. She wondered why she felt nervous on this beautiful Key West morning in 1918. Wasn't it just another day?

As she opened the door more than just bright morning light flooded into the room and her life. The small boy who stood before her had his head bowed like he was studying his dirty bare feet and didn't look up like he would have normally. He just stood there and mumbled, "Mornin' Miz Pinder. I been sent over here to bring you this telegram."

With that, he pulled the envelope from his pocket and offered it up, spun around, still not making eye contact but managed a gurgle sounding, "Bye, Miz Pinder."

Emily Pinder stood like a statue in the doorway holding the envelope in her now trembling hands until, through already misting eyes, she forced herself to look down and confirm her worst fear. It was from the War Department in Washington, D.C.

The Gang

I'm the only one left now which is funny because I wasn't the youngest of the gang we called the Black Mangrove Society. But life doesn't always go the way you think...that's one thing for sure.

I say 'we' called it the Black Mangrove Society but, like most everything we did back then as boys growing up in Key West, the whole idea was John "Bubba" Pinder's inspiration. It wasn't just because he was the oldest but he was clearly the smartest of us all and, believe me, he used his smarts to get us into a lot of stuff we wouldn't have done without him. Like the time some big shot came from Chicago to collect rare tropical fish and was going to pay a lot for them. We found one and when we couldn't find any more, we'd swim under the building at night into the pen where he was keeping all the fish and get the same one from that morning. He was all excited when we'd brought him four until he found out it was the same fish. Bubba's mom made us give the money back. But we got a good laugh out of it while it lasted. I didn't know it at the time, but those would be the best days of my life.

Bubba even gave each of us our names. No, I don't mean what we signed with at school, but the name everyone wound up calling you. Key West was like that back then. Most all the boys had names and even some of the girls. You prayed you didn't get stuck with a bad one like "Big Lips" or "Runt."

Of course, when Bubba took a liking to a kid and gave him his name it was always a good one that seemed to fit. Like Abner Sweeting who got called "Tweetie" because he was damn near always whistling. He was pretty good, too...hear a song once and whistle it perfect after.

Then there was Henry Salinero who got called "Coffee." I'm not sure whether it was because his family ran the grocery store where they served café con leche or because he was a kind of swarthy-looking Cuban kid. Bubba never explained why he picked the names except maybe once or twice when it was pretty obvious like when a seagull flew over and crapped on Joe Esquinaldo and, of course, he got to be called, "Poopy" for the rest of his life. It wasn't a bad thing though because back then getting crapped on by a bird was considered good luck by the Cubans, who, like the native Conchs, had a lot of funny ideas about such things.

"Yoyo" was just Yoyo because what else are you going to call someone named Jesus Arroyo? He could have got a lot worse. He was always in trouble for something. I guess Miss Marina, our first grade teacher, was right about it when she said anytime she had a kid named Jesus she knew he was going to be a problem!

Bubba called me "Tuffy." I was small for my age and it seemed I was always going at it with someone about something. Like I said Bubba never said why. My name is John Knowles.

The Meeting

"Bubba's dead," I said. "Don't you get it? He's dead and he ain't never coming back from that God damned war we all thought was so wonderful for him to lie about his age and go to."

I still remember the exact words I used to tell the fellows about the telegram I just delivered to Bubba's mother that morning. I knew what the telegram was because my father ran the Western Union office in Key West and I'd delivered a few like this one before. Believe me when I tell you, though, this one felt a whole lot different. I mean, of course, I knew all the families that got them. Everyone knew everyone then, but for Bubba it was different. He was more than the leader of the gang. He was like a big brother who would always step in for you in a fight. He was the guy who tried "it" first. Christ, he was our hero.

When he came home on leave in his uniform after basic training, we all went to meet him at the train station. It was like he was a returning general or something. And, of course, he didn't have to be the way he was with us then. He was a man now and we were still punk kids. He could have strutted off that train and had any girl he wanted and even gone into the bars for a beer. But no...that wasn't Bubba's way. He was as loyal as always and hugged us all like little brothers and made his easy jokes.

"Hey Poop, you keepin' your head down? Tuffy, I hope the other guy looks worse than you!"

Jesus, we felt like kings and everywhere Bubba went we all went. It was just like old times. We hung on every word of his stories about training camp and thought it was just the grandest of adventures.

Then the day came when Bubba's leave was over and his orders came. He was to ship out of New York to some place in France so he could go kill Krauts. We weren't too sure what a Kraut was except Mr. Altman, the baker, was one and I couldn't understand why we'd want to kill people like Mr. Altman. Bubba tried to explain about the president and countries and all, but we were just island people 120 miles from the mainland and 90 miles from Cuba. What did we know?

I remember waving goodbye to Bubba from the

platform. We were all shouting and yelling and Bubba was just standing there at the back of the last car looking swell in his uniform but with a funny look I'd never seen before. His mother was crying into the coat of Bubba's dad who was standing as stiff as a board.

The Tree

We were all crying now but we didn't care. It was us...the Society. It was for Bubba. Whoever said men aren't supposed to cry never lost anything worth a damn.

After a while of just staring blank faced and letting the reality of it sink in, Tweetie spoke first.

"What do you mean he ain't never coming home? Ain't they gonna even send his body back?"

"No," I said. "You know there's been a few other Key Westers kilt over there and some are probably just blown all to hell, but they never send anybody back anyway unless they're somebody important like a general or a rich guy. Mostly they just get buried wherever they are. No, Bubba is dead and buried in France and that's that."

The thought of Bubba being buried in some far away place hung in the air of the small shack we built for our clubhouse like the foul breath of reality that it was.

"Whaddya mean 'that's that'? 'That's that' is shit," Coffee wailed with tears, snot and spittle collecting and dripping off his quivering chin.

"Christ, Coffee, I didn't mean it like that but it's just the truth that's all."

"So 'that's that' means that someday somebody'll put his name on a goddamned plaque somewhere in the goddamned park, like the one for the guys who died in the Civil War?" Poopy managed to choke out wanting it to sound tougher than it did.

"Yeah, I guess," I said. "But that just don't seem like enough. I mean what about us? We're the Society and he was a brother. What are we going to do?"

"We ain't got any money for no plaque," said Tweetie. "And anyway, where'd we put it?"

Yoyo, who'd been sitting quiet now for a long time, suddenly drew everybody's attention when he stood up looking off into nothing and said, "I know exactly what Bubba would want. You know how everything in the Society is ours and nobody else's like this place, our handshake and secret code words – all the stuff he came up with to make us feel like blood brothers? Bubba'd want something that only we knew about that would be part of the Society...another bond sort of. He'd want us to plant a tree to remember him by so every time we went by it the people who meant the most to him would think of him. Yeah, a tree...a remembering tree! What do you say, guys?"

"That's it!"

"Yeah, a tree!"

"A mahogany tree!"

"Yeah, that's good!"

"A mahogany tree that'll grow a long time!"

We were shouting and laughing and crying all at the same time because we all knew Yoyo had got it right and it was something we could do to ease our pain.

The Ceremony
It was about a month after the telegram and the

church service that we all went over to the Pinders' house. We had been there a lot since the news and when we told Mr. and Mrs. Pinder about what we wanted to do, they said it was a fine idea and they'd like to have it in their yard where they could take care of it. Of course we agreed and today was the day.

For the previous couple of weeks we had scoured the hammocks for a suitable specimen and found a beauty over on Stock Island near the Indian Mounds. It was straight and healthy. We dug it up, being careful not to cut a single root and put it in a wash tub and brought it over across the channel to Key West in Poopy's little cat boat.

We didn't know about planting trees or anything but it seemed watering was all it needed because on the day it was to be planted it was healthy and fine. The hole was dug in the corner of the yard so you'd be able to see it from either street that made up their corner lot.

It was one of those magical days of autumn in October when the breeze was light, the skies were clear blue and the air was laden with the sweet smell of the sea and flowers. It was the kind of a day we'd have been doing something special with Bubba.

At the appointed time, we gathered around the hole and even Mrs. Pinder helped us lift the tree into the hole. We all pushed the dirt in with our hands patting it down snug around the roots.

This being done we stood in a circle and passed around a watering can so each of us could pour out a little water and say something.

We were all crying, of course. Mrs. Pinder more than anyone. Only Mr. Pinder held back, but I knew he wanted to.

The words weren't anything to remember. Just things like, "So long Bubba", "Goodbye, son", "I'm really going to miss ya, pal" and the like. But when it came to Tweetie, he poured the water from the can and then started to whistle *Taps* at which even Mr. Pinder broke down.

Believe me when I tell you it was the most beautiful thing I've ever heard before or since. When he finished we all joined hands and sang *Amazing Grace*, stood for a while in silence, and then just broke the circle and walked away without another word.

Now

Well, that's the story of the Remembering Tree, as it became known on the island. It was supposed to be just us but somehow it got out about the tree and I guess it's all right. Of course, I'm an old man now and every time I go by it I still think of Bubba. I started to think about the folks who were around then, who are either gone or dead now, and I don't know if anyone else even knows about the big mahogany tree on Frances Street. What good's a Remembering Tree if nobody remembers? Maybe I should ask the owners if I could put a sign on it? I wonder who lives there?

THE JUDAS GOAT

Julio Gomez hated the police. *Habaneros* wouldn't take the job because Havana was, after all, a big small town. So they brought in young, tough *campesinos* from the country who enjoyed the work. His ribs still hurt from the gratuitous beating he'd received from one of Fidel's thugs just three days ago for the crime of being in the wrong part of town without his papers. Ileana was somehow able to get him out of jail with a well-placed twenty dollars American and a flirtatious smile at the fat sergeant at the desk.

"*Que hola, mi amor?*" Ileana asked, trying to act cheerful at the sight of her boyfriend in his rumpled, unshaven humiliation.

"*Que hola?* Oh *bien*, just Goddamned *bien*. How do you think I am? Three days in a cell with a hundred stinking men, one toilet and food, if you can call it that, once a day ... if they remember. Where have you been? Why didn't someone come sooner?"

"No one knew," she said, casting her eyes down.

"Yeah, I guess another Cuban in jail wasn't exactly big news. I mean, we do need to keep Havana looking right for the *touristas*."

Of all the indignities and all the privations, the charade played out in Havana irked Julio Gomez the most. Havana wasn't for the *habaneros*. It was a show for tourists. The once elegant city, even in its tattered state of decay, was beautiful, at least architecturally. And sure, if you had dollars there was food, good food and plenty of it, at the privately run *paladars* in people's homes. This breach of the socialist manifesto was a necessary evil in Castro's show city. The government could never run anything like a restaurant that required skill, hard work and dedicated labor ... the corruption would wreck it before a glass of water hit the table. Besides, they got a hefty piece of the action. And the bars at the Segovia or Floridita, where Hemingway used to drink, or the Nacional and the Copa Cabana ... if you were Cuban, forget it. The only occupations were to serve the state in menial subsistence work or some humiliating job in tourism. The worst was the legion of young girls who sold themselves to feed their families. No, thought Julio bitterly, Havana, "the pearl of the Antilles," the city of culture and music and laughter was definitely not for Cubans.

Julio worked as a guide in one of the cigar factories set up for tourists. He had a knack for languages and his English was good enough for the job. He loved his work because the entire place served to confirm his smoldering distrust and resentment for all things government and the wretches who pandered to it for the crumbs swept off the table of its largesse. He loved it because every day he could play a game where one day he screwed the government and the next the fat, loud tourists in their clown clothes. Today it was the government's turn.

"Now please, before we start our tour," Julio was saying to a group of ten tourists made up of Americans, Canadians and Germans, "please, two things I must ask of you. First, please, no photos in the factory and second, please do not try to buy cigars from the workers. On the last tour we had a big problem, no?" His eye darted to his supervisor, an officious, middle aged man with veined, wrinkled skin that looked like bleached tobacco leaf. When he nodded his approval, Julio turned and motioned for the group to follow.

It wasn't five minutes into the tour when Julio caught, out of the corner of his eye, a worker tugging on the sleeve of the trailing member of the group and holding up five fingers on one hand and one on the other hand, silently intoning, "five cigars, one dollar". The tourist pulled away shaking his head no, only to encounter the worker at the next table offering ten for a dollar.

Julio smiled a sardonic smile and, of course, did nothing about this little act of revolution against the revolution. He knew the tourist was afraid because rules were different here. Despite the veil of order this was, after all, a police state. If you got caught doing something, who were you going to call, the concierge at your hotel?

"Right this way, please," said Julio. "Gather around, please."

The small group gathered around one of fifty wrapping tables in the large room. There was an elevated stage at the front with a small desk and a single wooden chair. A microphone on the desk was for the readers. Every day while the workers made cigars the readers would read *Granma*, the newspaper named after the boat that brought Fidel and his followers to the island in 1958. They also read books or played music, anything to make the time pass in the tedious monotony of rolling cigars. The man at the table didn't look up when the group gathered around his table. He'd seen this a thousand times and what did he care about tourists anyway?

"This is Martin, ladies and gentlemen. He is placing the filler tobacco in these presses here. They will take their form and then be wrapped in special leaf and trimmed."

Julio surveyed the faces of his audience and knew it was the moment. Making sure no supervisors were in sight he said in a low voice, "Ok, anyone want to take a picture? Go ahead. It's okay here."

At first the tourists didn't know what to do.

"No, really, it's okay. Go ahead."

"You sure?" asked one of the American tourists.

"Yes, here is okay," answered Julio in a furtive tone, knowing full well that there wasn't a soul in the place who gave a damn whether the tourists took pictures or not. It was just a well practiced ruse of the guides to get tips. Of course, the guides had to kick back part of the money but that was how the game was played. And no one played it better than Julio Gomez.

Trading cameras back and forth, the tourists clicked away. They snapped the stage, the workers, each other with Julio and every possible combination until Julio knew the moment was played out. He was a master of his art.

"Okay, folks, please, let's move on." Satisfied by their little bit of defiance of the revolution in getting what they were sure was a rare photo, the group moved obediently after their leader.

"Here is where the cigars are boxed, the final part of their journey, so to speak."

Looking about in his practiced furtive manner, Julio whispered, "Anybody want to buy cigars? Is okay here. Ramon is a friend," he said, nodding to the lanky young man standing behind the weathered work table.

Ramon smiled revealing a mouth of perfectly white teeth, one of which was dramatically capped in gold.

"Que hola Julio? Quantos quieres?"

"He asks me how many you want," repeated Julio in English.

"I thought we weren't supposed to buy cigars in here," said one of the group.

"Is okay here," shrugged Julio.

"Ramon is, how do you say, cool? In the store you will pay twenty American dollars but here only five. You just don't get the box. You must put them in your pockets."

The bills came out and cigars that weren't *Cohibas* but had the *Cohiba* labels were stuffed into pockets, camera cases and purses until no more would fit without being too obvious. Julio knew that the supervisors knew but they didn't care. As long as they got their cut, so what? After all, they weren't paid enough to even put decent food on the table. Up the chain someone knew that the supervisors knew. That Julio knew. They all knew. The thought made Julio laugh out loud at the absurdity of the revolutionary order.

The tour ended with everyone happy at the success of his part of the little charade that would repeat itself every thirty minutes throughout the day. Revolution in Cuba was alive and well, though probably not exactly the way Fidel had planned it.

Julio left the factory feeling better than he had that

morning. He could feel the bulge of American and Canadian dollars and Euros in his pants pockets. All in all not a bad day he thought to himself. Good money, a little revenge and a cool, clear evening to walk the Malecon with Ileana. Maybe he'd even get lucky tonight. Then he saw him.

Their eyes met too quickly for Julio to hide. It was Carlos, the same cop who had beaten him and thrown him in jail last week. He was a sadist who relished his well deserved reputation on the streets of Havana. He was a tough on his way up in the department and he knew how to play the game.

"*Oye, chico, que hola?*" Carlos mocked as he made his way directly to Julio.

Julio's good cheer faded and his heart sank.

"*Bien, Jeffe, y usted?*" Julio responded with as much formality and respect as the bile in his throat would permit. He knew even as his words came out they sounded false but it only made Carlos laugh and snarl back, "The *Jeffe* is great. How did you enjoy the station's hospitality, *cabron*? Food and a roof over your head, eh?"

Julio didn't answer. He knew it wasn't a question of interest but a picking of the scab of idignity.

"Oye, you know, it's good I run into you tonight. I have actually been looking for you."

"Oh yeah, why?"

"Well I figure maybe you want to do me a favor, that's why. You know, maybe you don't want me asking for your papers tonight which, even if you learned your lesson and you have them, I might drop them or something. Or maybe you might have trouble finding them in that wad of cash you got in your pocket. Or, hey, I saw that pretty girlfriend waiting for you at the Malecon. I wonder, does she have her papers? You know what I mean, *cabron?*"

A sick knot twisted in Julio's stomach. "Yeah, I think I understand. What do you want?"

"Not much, *cabron.* Some information maybe. Like how I know what you got in your pockets, I know other things. For example, I hear some of those *madecones* at the shit hole where you work are thinking they are going to take a cruise to Miami next week. You know anything about that, Gomez?"

There was always talk about leaving but it was talk that could really fuck your life up so unless you were directly in a group it was mainly just rumors until it happened.

"No man, you know, people are always talking about such things but I don't know nothing about any plans."

Carlos reached forward and slowly took hold of Julio's shirt and pulled his face to within a couple inches and growled in a low voice that made Julio's blood cold, "*Mierda hombre,* I know you hate my guts and to me you're less than dog *mierda.* Somebody's planning something and if they do it and I don't know about it, I'm going to blame someone. And that someone's you." With that he brought his knee up hard between Julio's legs. Julio's legs buckled and he crumpled to the sidewalk gasping for air.

Carlos squatted down beside him resting his thick forearms on his thighs. A smile opened on a mouth full of tobacco stained teeth pocked with rot.

As he spoke, Julio could feel Carlos' hand pulling the

bills out of his pocket. "Don't worry, *hombre*. I'm not going to take it all ... just half. What I really want you're going to give me later. You talk to that *hijo de puta* Ramon and tell him you want to go with him, and if he says he doesn't know what you're talking about you tell him you're going or nobody's going. You got it, *cabron*?"

Julio managed a weak, "*Si*".

"That's what I thought you'd say. You find out and I'll talk with you in a few days, say day after tomorrow in front of the Nacional at eight. *Adios, Chico.*"

Julio lay there a few minutes ignoring the furtive stares of passersby. In Castro's Cuba you kept your eyes and your mouth shut. When he could stand he got up and staggered home. He was in no mood or condition to see Ileana. He hated Carlos. He hated himself.

The next day, at the end of the fourth tour, Julio caught Ramon coming out of the men's room on his way to lunch.

"*Oye*, Ramon, I need to talk with you."

"*Como no*, Julio. Come with me to lunch."

The small café was the typical hole-in-the-wall place. There was rarely much available except for beans and rice. Most Cubans couldn't afford any restaurant no matter how meager; however, if you were in a line of work that generated foreign currency, you were always welcome.

The two men selected an out-of-the-way corner table. Not that it mattered. They were the only two in the place. After ordering, Ramon spoke, "So *que quieres*, what do you want?"

"Look, I'm not going to beat around the bush. I want

to go with you. I'm sick of this place."

"Go where?" answered Ramon, first startled, then suspicious.

"Don't fuck with me. You've got a group together and you're leaving. I want to go."

Ramon didn't answer but sat in confused silence. This was not like borrowing some sugar or asking a favor. This was putting your life in someone's hands.

"What makes you think I'm planning something anyway?" he finally said, probing.

"I just know, that's all. Call it a hunch, but the way you're acting now confirms it."

"Look, even if I was, you know there might be other people involved. It's never just one."

"So talk to them."

"Why should I? How do you know how much has gone into the plan? How's it right for you just to come because you say so? I know you got roughed up by Carlos but that's not enough reason."

"How did you know about that?"

"Like you, I just know."

"I hate Cuba. I hate my life. I'm sick of the *fabrica* and assholes like Carlos. I can help. Another man is good, no? I've got money. Look, now that I know, you can't afford not to let me go if you get my meaning."

"Are you threatening me, Julio?"

"No, just saying what's obvious. I'm fed up. I'm desperate."

"Desperate enough to leave your family? How about Ileana?"

After the briefest of moments, "Yeah, I am. I don't

have much family left and Ileana is just a convenience."

"You're a cold one, *hombre*."

"So when's the day?"

"I have to speak with the others."

"Do it soon. I wouldn't want to wake up one day and not see you at the *fabrica*," he said as he stood and tossed some bills on the table.

"Tomorrow morning, Ramon. I want an answer tomorrow morning." He left quickly. Though he hadn't eaten all day, he felt like he was about to throw up. How could this be happening. *Un raton* for Carlos ... how could he be so low? It was Ramon or him he rationalized. That's the way it was. Viva Cuba.

The next morning Julio had more on his mind than who to screw this day. He already knew. He found Ramon out on the loading dock smoking a cigar.

"*Que hola?*" said Julio just to announce his presence.

Ramon didn't answer. He spit and threw his half smoked Churchill after it.

"Okay, you're in. I spoke to the group. You have to put in $100 American and be ready with 24 hours notice. Can you do that and keep your mouth shut?"

"*Si*, I can do that, but why don't you have a date?"

"And no questions. You're in, but the plan is already set. The less you know the better they feel. They're not happy but I vouched for you."

"How many are in the group?"

"You don't listen too good. Don't make me sorry about this, Julio. I need the money today for expenses."

With that Ramon turned, thrust his hands in his pockets and walked back into the *fabrica*. Julio shrugged and followed.

It was past eight but Julio couldn't leave. Carlos would come when he felt like it. Julio sat and watched the odd collection of vintage American cars and newer Russian cars made into taxis arrive and depart the entrance of the Nacional. Fat tourists in flowered shirts with cameras came and went in a stream that left Julio to ponder the what ifs. What if he really did take off to Miami? Life here filled him with disgust. He had dreams that would never come true in Cuba. What if he got caught? Carlos would make sure his life would be hell on earth. What if he got away? What would happen to his family and as little as he cared about Ileana, he didn't want to think about what Carlos would do to her. He was trapped no matter what he ...

The hard slap on his back caused him to fall forward off the low wall he was on and then struggled to remain upright. He knew without looking it was Carlos.

"*Que hola, Julio*? Sorry I'm late, I was getting laid," he smirked. "So what do you know?"

Julio hesitated for one last moment before he went all in. "Alright, there is a plan, you were right."

"I knew it!" Carlos exclaimed, slapping Julio again on the shoulder. This is going to get me promoted *Cabron*! Hey, *amigo*, don't look so unhappy. There's something in it for you too. Five hundred American. So ... when are those *putos* going?"

"I don't know yet. They won't tell me until twenty four hours before."

Carlos' face fell then turned into a snarl. His fist caught Julio in the solar plexus so all he saw were stars as he doubled over to the ground.

"You *madecon*! You mess with me and I'll fuck you up!"

He started to raise his fist to strike Julio who was now on his knees but Julio raised a hand and gasped, "No, wait!"

Carlos stopped in mid swing. "Talk and talk fast, *cabron!*"

"Look, I'm telling you the truth. If I press for answers, I'm out. The only reason I think they're not talking is that it's soon."

Carlos was an animal, a dumb brute but cunning in human frailty. He was a meat eater and when he smelled blood, his perception became as sharp as splintered glass. He relaxed as Julio struggled for breath and staggered to his feet.

"Okay, okay, *chico*. I believe you. You know why? Because you lie to me, if I don't get you I'm going to get your brother, your uncle and, oh yeah, that pretty little girlfriend of yours."

He grabbed Julio's shirt hard enough to rip it and pulled him so close that Julio could smell the metallic rankness of his breath. He barked into Julio's face so that Julio's eye lashes twitched to the rhythm of his words, "You understand me, *cabron?*"

"Si," was all Julio could manage before the vomit came coursing out of his mouth onto the chest of Carlos' uniform.

Julio only heard a few words before his world turned black. When he awoke he had a lump on his head and was choking on a piece of paper stuck in his mouth. Once he finally composed himself he opened it to find only a phone number written in a heavy scrawl. He vomited.

"Man, you look like *mierda*. What happened to you?" Ramon was asking when Julio showed up at the *fabrica*.

"That's why I want to get out of this place. I got beat up last night. When are we going?"

Ramon sucked in his breath, pursed his lips and answered simply, "Tomorrow, ten o'clock from the beach just north of the Miramar Club. Bring nothing. If you're late don't bother showing up."

There was no joy this day for Julio. He just wanted it to be over. Ramon cautioned him to show up for work the next day and not act differently from any other day. He called the number Carlos had given him and got instructions to meet him that night in front of the Segovia at nine. The prospect weighed heavily enough on Julio that even the supervisor asked him if he was sick.

This time Carlos was waiting for him. He was in an unmarked car across the street from the hotel entrance. He spotted Julio first as he rounded the corner and waved him over.

"Get in," he commanded as Julio got within range.

Carlos accelerated away from the curb before Julio had the door closed. He didn't go far, just to a side street with no lights where no one would see them. Julio's heart was pounding.

"So, tomorrow at ten, eh?"

"Yeah, at the beach just ..."

"Yeah, you told me."

"How will you arrest them?" said Julio weakly.

"You mean 'us', don't you?" Carlos came back.

Julio's heart thumped.

"What do you mean, us?"

You're going to go there with them, *cabron*."

"Wait a minute, you never said anything about me going with them."

"I'm doing you a favor, *hombre*. If you don't show up, everyone's going to know who ratted them out."

"Don't use that word. You're making me do this."

"Look, *cabron,* I grew up in the meat business in the country. When the animals were brought in to the slaughter house we always had a Judas goat. He was trained to walk ahead of the herd so they wouldn't get nervous. Then, at the last minute, we'd pull him away and take care of the rest."

"So, that's the plan? We all show up at ten and you come and arrest us and then let me go?"

"Well, sort of. I'll be there earlier with three men. I've already been there and seen the boat. There's only one road in and we can hide in the car. We'll move in after everybody's on board so they don't scatter. You throw your hands up first so maybe everyone else will too. I don't want to kill anyone. The fun will come later at the station. Who knows how many *ratones* we might catch in one trap?"

Julio's stomach went cold. He knew what "fun at the station" meant.

"You wear a red shirt, OK? My men will put you in a separate car."

Julio started to get out but Carlos grabbed his wrist in a vise-hard grip. "Don't fuck this up, *cabron*. You hear me?" Julio nodded and Carlos released his arm with a smile. "Don't worry, *hombre*. I'll take care of everything."

Julio didn't sleep at first. He lay in his own sweat as thoughts of what would happen ran through his mind like a bad movie. The fan overhead clicked out a three-part rhythm that finally started saying in his brain, "Don't do this, don't do this, don't do this." He fell asleep an hour before the sun came up but he knew what he had to do.

Julio had to struggle to act out the day at *fabrica*. He even did the 'screw the government' routine with Ramon with whom he exchanged only furtive glances through the day. A few extra dollars might come in handy and if he didn't, the supervisor might get suspicious.

Julio was ready since there's not much preparation needed when you're told to 'bring nothing'. He had written letters to his brother, uncle and Ileana hoping to explain; and, if it all went bad, the letters would be found and they would be less likely to have any problems with the authorities.

The one thing Julio did bring was the old, army Colt his father had left him. Private guns were illegal but Julio had kept it anyway. His father had taught him to use it and he still had twenty rounds of bullets.

It was only seven o'clock but as soon as the sun went down, Julio left and went to the rendezvous point. He'd been to this beach cove many times and knew it well. The boat was on the shore and there was no sign of anyone else. Julio hid himself at the entrance of the road and waited.

At 8:30 a car approached turning off its lights as it pulled off onto the side road. It came within six feet of Julio who could now make out it was the police with

Carlos driving. Carlos stopped the car where the road came on to the beach then backed it into a thicket he had for the purpose of having the car lights aimed at the boat. After the engine shut off, the men pulled bushes up and over the car. Then it became deadly quiet.

Julio knew what he had planned but that was last night after drinks. Now was reality. Now was life and death in the balance. From somewhere in the recesses of his memory echoed Hemingway's, "The mark of a man is doing what he says drunk the next day when he's sober."

Julio massaged the old pistol in both hands, rose and approached the car. He could smell the tobacco smoke from the car. Salty sweat dripped off his upper lip into a dry mouth. Every step sounded like he was walking on dry sticks no matter how hard he tried for quiet.

"*Que hola, hombres?*" said Julio with as much false bravado as he could muster.

"What the hell are you doing here?" Carlos said as he tried to turn, only to find a .45 caliber pistol pressed to his temple.

"Anybody moves you die first, *amigo*. Alright everybody, put your hands out in front of you. Do it now!"

Slowly, eight hands extended. One by one Julio had them give over their weapons. First, he handcuffed them one to the other, and then through the steering wheel. All except Carlos. Carlos he pulled from the car then marched him off beyond ear shot of the others and cuffed him to a tree. Carlos watched him return to the car and then return after a few minutes.

"What'd you do, *cabron*? Do you have any idea what kind of trouble you're in?"

"Yeah, I pretty much know and just in case I don't get another chance ..." With that he laid the pistol across Carlos' face as hard as he could.

Carlos spat blood and teeth and hissed, "You hit like a woman but that's okay. You let me go now and finish this business and I'll mark us up as even."

"Not a chance. You know what I told your buddies in the car? I told them about what a Judas goat is and how you set this up so you could go with us. Now, when I dump your sorry ass off shore, they'll be waiting for you to explain how they got locked up and you got taken in the boat. You like that story, *cabron*?"

It didn't take much to convince the group to take Carlos along because with the cops locked in the car watching, they didn't have much choice. About a mile off shore they gave Carlos an empty five gallon plastic jug and let Ileana push him into the cold, dark Atlantic water to be alone with his thoughts about "fun at the station".

SECOND CHANCES

"The stupid bastard," thought Manning as he looked down from his tree top sniper position at the small black pajama clad man leaning up against the same tree. "The first thing they tell you is not to smoke in the jungle and there he goes on his second cigarette."

He could already smell the acrid smoke hanging in the still, gelatinous air of sector 8 Quang Tri Province, Viet Nam. Smoke in the jungle will remain for hours and it's like a neon sign that says, "Come and get it".

Jack Manning knew this and a lot more he wished he didn't. This was his second tour, a fact he still couldn't sort out. The first time he was on fire to go to Viet Nam and fight for his country just like his dad in WWII. But any thoughts this war was about truth or honorable were quickly dispelled by the numbing corruption in Saigon and the horrific reality of the battle field.

Jack Manning was a farm boy whose whole existence had been dedicated to the ritual of life. His father had taught him the mysteries and beauty of renewal through the birth and death of the farm animals and the sowing and reaping of crops. It was right and clean and understandable. Even death on the farm was natural and good. Here there was no redemption in death and killing. Here, it was a sick, twisted black hole of confusion.

Maybe he'd come back this second time because he couldn't believe the first time was the way it was supposed to be and what he had done could in some way be redeemed. Maybe the young hippie girl at the airport who spit in his face and screamed "baby killer" at him had made him angry enough to make him want to think he was right. Maybe he liked it.

Manning shook off these thoughts for this was no time to be distracted. In the rest of the world it was, "You snooze, you lose". Here, you were dead. The fact was, he was a natural. The Sniper Corp preferred farm boys. They were comfortable with firearms. They were used to long solitary hours. They seemed more at ease with killing. They didn't hesitate.

Manning studied the high-powered Winchester model 70 .03-.06 rifle with its high tech 8x Unertl scope cradled in his lap like a sleeping animal. As his eyes passed over the camouflaged carcass of his weapon, a deadly calm came upon him. He had fifteen kills out of fifteen shots with this rifle. This ratio was the whole pride of the elite Sniper Corp; they would sometimes be on a site for a week just to take one shot. If you missed, you didn't talk about it.

The Sniper Corps was divided into two camps. On the one side were the "yahoos". They were the young punks whacked out on drugs. They did this because they liked it. Most of them hand loaded their own ammo adding extra grains of powder and using hollow head bullets filled with mercury. When the round hit a human head at 2000 feet a second, the effect of the expanding mercury made it like a bowling ball hitting a watermelon.

In the other camp were technicians like the legendary Carlos Hathcock. They did this because it needed doing. There was a standing $8.00 bounty on snipers. Hathcock, respectfully nicknamed "Long Tra'ng" for the white feather he always wore, carried a $1,000 price on his head for ninety-five confirmed kills. Manning had met him once and was taken with his quiet, self-effacing manner. He liked how Hathcock said, "it was just a job and it saved a lot of our men's lives." Manning needed to believe in something like that. Yes, he was good at it but killing gnawed at him and he wanted desperately to understand it. The sniper motto, "Do it right the first time," wasn't enough.

With excruciating lizard slowness born of the habits of survival, Manning moved to examine his prey. Slow ... first move the eyes then the head. Reserve all body movements unless absolutely necessary. Slow ... careful. Don't brush against anything. Not a leaf, twig or drop of sweat must fall that might possibly cause detection, flight or your own death. Slow ... so slow and quiet you wonder if he can hear your pounding heart.

"What's he doing? Is that a wallet? Yeah, the dumb shit is sitting down there having a smoke looking at pictures of his kids! Gotta respect these little bastards though ... first the French and now us dumping enough ordinance on the place to take out California and they're still here. I don't care how many bodies they say – we ain't winning this war. If we're winning how come I'm seeing more patrols than last time? No, the blood we spill is like rain on a new field that sprouts shoots faster than we can mow them."

"Wait a minute, what's he doing? Christ! He's putting a pistol in his mouth ... he's gonna blow himself away! Well come on, boy, pull the trigger. Come on, just do it.

Save me the trouble. Can't do it, huh?" Manning watched with confused detachment as the man threw the gun from him and dropped his face into his hands and wept.

Jack Manning watched the man recede from the tree they had shared like a space of time created by a decision that's yet to be made. At 50 yards, he slowly put the Winchester into position. At 75 yards he had the cross hairs of the scope dead on the back of the man's head. At 100 yards he decided there was no need for wind compensation and clicked off the safety. He wrapped his finger around the trigger and drew a breath. As the little man disappeared into the jungle Jack Manning exhaled, clicked on the safety and knew it was time to go home.

MOTHER'S DAY

The clear plastic I.V. bag hanging by Wilma Garth's bed did its work in silence. As she studied it, it seemed to her the drops fell in slow motion down into the tube attached to her arm and she had begun to imagine each drop made a splashing sound though she knew they didn't. Wilma Garth thought to herself how the mind plays tricks on you when you're sick. She still remembered the time when she was nine years old and had a fever of 104 degrees for two days. She had drifted in and out of strange confusing dreams of oversized proportions and realizations of the coming and goings of family and doctors.

Wilma had never owned a TV and now the oxygen tent made her beloved books impossible so that all there was to do was watch the I.V., think and wait for the periodic visits of the crisp, efficient nurses and serious faced doctors.

"Good morning Mrs. Garth," chirped the ICU first shift nurse. "Did you sleep well?" Wilma was vaguely aware that the tube in her arm was being removed.

Oh yes, dearie, Wilma thought to herself, "I have tubes in my arm, tubes between my legs, tubes in my mouth and tubes in my nose. Someone wakes me up every hour to make sure I can still wake up. Yes, I had a wonderful sleep. Why in the name of Pete does she ask me questions she knows I can't answer? She must be studying to be a dentist. She is a lovely child though, so fresh and full of life and still with an intact sense of what she's doing. They must pick only the best to be in this part of the hospital.

The way she cocks her head when she smiles reminds me of my best friend Julia when we were kids growing up on the farm just outside of Asheville. Just days before she passed away 10 years ago I remember we talked about how close we were back then. Momma used to say we were like two peas in a pod and I guess she was right. I can still see us...pigtails, bib overalls and I don't think we ever wore shoes except to Church and school. We did everything together and were best friends our whole lives.

Time is such an odd thing. It seems like it all happened just yesterday but at the time it felt like it would never end. I remember the warm lazy summer days were filled with church picnics, swimming in the creek, catching lightning bugs, eating spring house cooled watermelon, and sitting on the porch after dinner listening to the adults tell stories and laugh. Sometimes daddy would bring out his guitar and sing. His songs were always slow and romantic and I remember when he was singing it was like he and momma were the only two people there.

I remember harvest time in the autumn being better than any birthday. There was an air of excited expectation of fulfillment and everybody and everything was a part of a great ritual of life that was defined, not by us, but by the urgency of the season. I remember we all worked but it never felt like work and the smell of freshly mowed fields in the day gave way at night to long hours of sorting the apples or laying up vegetables. Our farm had peaches, plums, apples, wild raspberries, wheat, corn, beans and potatoes. We churned our own butter and collected our own eggs. I remember going to the store was mostly for clothes and tools and treats and to socialize. I felt safe. I remember time seemed to be measured out to us in a way that we could understand...I remember, I remember.

"There, I think we got all your plumbing straightened out," said the nurse in a vain attempt at humor. "Doctor Cason will be here short...oh, here he is now. Good morning Doctor," she said straightening perceptibly.

"Good morning, Jane, and how is our Mrs. Garth?"

"I think she looks much better this morning!" said nurse Jane with a little too much good cheer.

"Well, let's just take a look," said the young doctor as he picked up the metal clipboard hanging at Wilma's feet.

Yes, you do that sonny. Study the charts, numbers and dosages and tell me how this 96-year-old body is coming right around and how I'll be square dancing by Saturday.

I don't know how a body could be this kind of doctor. I've been around birthing and dying of farm animals and country people all my life and it always seemed when it was time everybody just knew it and it happened and it was good and clean and right. I've been here for three days and watched the agonized last attempts to cling to a few more minutes that are traded for a lifetime of dignity.

He's a good man though. I think he cares and believes he's doing right. God knows there're precious few good men and almost none that understand life. I thought my daddy was the only one until I met Robert Joseph

125

Garth...my Bobby Joe.

In his whole life I was the only one he'd let call him Bobby Joe. It was Robert to everyone else. I remember Bobby Joe came into my life when I was 17 and my whole world turned over forever. One day I was a tall skinny kid whose best friend was a girl and the next I was a woman whose instincts told her it was time to no longer be a girl and all the things that come with that knowledge. Bobby Joe was 18. He was the best of them all ... and there were a few. He was tall, lean, and strong but he was gentle, kind and smart about life and living. It wasn't that he picked me or I picked him. We just knew from the beginning we'd always be together.

I remember sitting on the porch one night watching our kids in the yard catching lightning bugs. I looked around at the same porch from where I grew up, at a good man on a clear beautiful mountain evening with its symphony of crickets, frogs and laughing children and I knew...I knew with the greatest certainty you can have that I was where I should be at the center of the universe as I knew it.

We had two children and the joy of watching the changes as they grew up like when I took Little Bobby to school on the first day and when his teacher took his hand he was still holding on to mine so that when she started to walk away he became suspended on his tiptoes between us. He hung there for the briefest moment then my baby slipped off my hand into the realm of boyhood. But life doesn't always work out in your own terms. Our son was killed in Viet Nam. Bobby was always a good little boy and he was a fine young man like his dad. I can only take solace in the fact that his 20 years on this earth were good ones which is more than I can say for some who have had more time. But I'll be damned if I'll ever forgive those who wasted his beautiful life.

Something went out of Bobby Joe after that. Life was still good but he didn't seem to laugh as much. When Katie had the grandchildren a little came back but he was never the same again. I buried him six months ago and I miss him.

"Good morning, Ms. Lyda," said the receptionist nurse to Katie Lyda as she made her way across the spartan intensive care unit waiting room. Katie was only vaguely aware that the single strand of tinsel garland reminded her that it was Christmas morning.

"Hi, Renee," lilted Katie in her native Carolina accent. "How is she?"

"I know she had a bad night but I swear she is one strong lady. I've never seen anybody take so much and not complain, cry or even moan."

"Yes," said Katie, "she's always been that way ever since I can remember. She had my little brother at home in the morning and made dinner for the family that night. Can I see her?"

"Yes, dear, Dr. Cason just left. You can go right in."

Renee watched as Katie pushed through the *Restricted Access* swinging doors of ICU and disappeared into the world of last hopes. She turned back to her stack of charts with a sigh of acceptance earned over five years of dealing with the emotional highs and lows of the ICU. She was only slightly aware that about 20 minutes had passed and Katie was standing in front of her desk.

"Leaving already?" Renee asked a little puzzled.

"I think you better come with me," Katie said flatly, "my momma has passed on."

Renee's eyes darted instinctively to the life support monitors and gasped at the flat line on the Wilma Garth's screen.

"Christ!" she gasped as she leaped to her feet. "How could..."

"Don't hurry," Katie stopped her, "it's over. It's okay".

Without another word Renee walked quickly through the swinging doors down the hall and into the dimly lit room of Wilma Garth.

"She was like that when I came in," said Katie from behind the dumb struck nurse, "isn't she beautiful?"

There before them lay Wilma Garth supine on fluffed pillows like she was in a deep tranquil sleep. Scattered around the floor were I.V. tubes and hissing respirators like so many cast off snakes. A single bulb above her head cast a small circle of light over her face that made her white hair into a translucent halo...and she was smiling.

"THE SHOE SHINE"

I was 15 minutes early to my five o'clock meeting and remembered there was a shoeshine stand around back of the ornate brass Art Deco elevator by the newspaper stand. It was an important meeting with an investor I'd been referred to for a line of credit I sorely needed for my new business. A shoeshine was a luxury and something I probably should have done at home but things like that are usually an afterthought for me. The trivial fact of scuffed and dusty shoes yesterday took on whole a new meaning as part of the positive impression I hoped to make in the next 15 minutes.

I was cheered to see no one else waiting and climbed up on the elevated platform to take my seat in a surprisingly comfortable chair. I remember thinking to myself how the chairs for shoeshine stands are, in fact, universally comfortable. Was it part of the deal or the fact that you're sitting above the world while someone performs the lowliest personal service left in today's detached world? I wasn't sure as I picked up a well-read copy of the news with only a vague awareness that the shoeshine "boy" was taking his seat in front of me.

"Would you like the regular shine or the Spencer Super Shine?" I heard a smooth clear resonant voice ask. I put down my paper with a "Huh?"

"Would you like the regular shine or the Spencer Super Shine?" the man now sitting in front of me patiently inquired.

"Uh, what's the difference?" I asked now a little unsure of myself as I found myself staring at the most astonishingly handsome face I had ever seen. His face was remarkable for the clear skin of slightly olive complexion framed with jet black hair combed straight back into a neat trim at the neck. But the eyes . . . pale sky blue expressionless orbs set in white marble that seemed like they could rivet the attention of anyone the young man chose.

"What's the matter?" he said through a knowing smile that exposed straight white teeth. It was said in a practiced way meant to disarm those he was addressing.

"Uh, uh, nothing," I stammered somewhat embarrassed. "What's a Spencer Super Shine?" I inquired lamely.

"Oh, it's a kind of trademark shine I do here. The regular is $2.50 and the Spencer is $4. I hand melt the final coat of wax. It gives a better shine and lasts twice as long as the regular." His pitch was earnest but a take it or leave it offer of better value.

"How long does a Spencer take?" I asked.

"About ten minutes," he replied.

"Alright, give me the Spencer. If it's what you say maybe I won't have to worry about forgetting to shine my own shoes for a while."

"Yes," he replied as he opened a well worn wooden drawer at the bottom of the platform. "Most people don't appreciate the value of a good shine these days. It makes the leather wear longer and it has the advantage of being a little something that makes you feel better. Pretty good deal in today's world for four bucks, wouldn't you say?"

"Uh, yes, yes. I guess I never thought of it like that."

"Well, like I said, most people don't. But, I guarantee you'll be happy with your investment," he said as he bent to his task without further comment. I put my paper down.

His hands went through the procedures of brush, soap, stain, wax and buff, with a deftness we have long since ceased to appreciate in today's world. I was aware there was something strange about what he was doing and then it struck me that it was his hands. They were not the stained, cracked skin with broken, dirty nails I would have imagined. They were, in fact, elegant. The back of his muscular hands were covered with fine unblemished skin from which emanated long fingers, with manicured nails, adorned by a single gold ring on the little finger of his right hand. The ring was a crest of some sort but the distance and movements of his hand disallowed any recognition of its significance.

Like your barber, the relationship between you and a common bootblack always seems to permit an easy familiarity for discussions of politics, sports and even personal things. Thus emboldened, I asked, "May I ask you a question?"

"Sure," he replied, looking up in such a way that I suspected he was anticipating this inquiry.

"Don't take this the wrong way," I started, "but you don't look like a typical bootblack."

He looked up again with a wry chuckle and said, "I'm not. I only do this half a day once a week."

"Really," my interest growing by the moment, "what else do you do, if you don't mind me asking?"

"Not at all," he said never looking up from the wax-melt Spencer Shine that he was applying, but I had completely forgotten about. "I am an investor of sorts." Being encouraged by his ready answer, I pressed on further into business which was certainly not mine.

"Look," I said, "I'm more than a little curious. The investors I know are white-collar guys who play golf half days once a week. Why do you do this?"

For just a moment, the frenetic motion of his hands stopped, as though he were pondering his answer or, if he would answer at all. Then, without looking up, his hands took up the rhythmic buffing motion.

"I went to Harvard and then took my MBA at the Wharton School. I had some scholarships but my father would never let me work saying I needed all the time I had for study. My father worked as a bootblack at this stand in this building until the day he died. I work here for the love of him and to honor his memory."

Time stopped and I could feel my heart beating.

"All done sir. That'll be four dollars for the Spencer Super Shine."

I was startled back from my thoughts so quickly I could only mutter, "Thank you," and proffered the required four dollars with a dollar tip which he accepted with a gracious, "Thank you."

I could hardly get the last ten minutes out of my mind as I made my way to the Penthouse Suite 2400 for my appointment. I stopped dead in my tracks and looked at the door with a knowing smile when I read the sign...

SPENCER INVESTMENTS
SPENCER BUILDING

TWO MEN

They lived on a boat, the father and his son. This in itself was highly unusual, even for Key West. These weren't passing-through rich people on their yachts or hippies in worn out, going-no-place sailboats. They were living in Key West on a boat. The mother had long since departed for greener pastures (or at least a man with a steady job) and C.B. McCabe and Little C.B. were living on a boat in the basin behind Christmas Tree Island which shielded them from both the glitz and lights of the waterfront and unexpected nor'easters.

From the now-gone glory days of turtles, sponges, shrimp and fish, C.B. was still known as "King Of The Spongers", a name he proudly proclaimed to any who would listen to his tales. Some were fascinated. Some just rolled their eyes because they didn't get it. The father and son washed in captured rain water on board the small wooden motorsailer, Eileen, where they also ate most of their meals of fish, conch and anything else the sea would yield to the practiced hands of C.B.

Every morning at precisely 5:00 am, the old man would rise - whether the sun did or not - to make sure the boy had proper clothes for school and a hearty breakfast of boiled fish, eggs and grits.

Then at 7:00 the small johnboat was loaded with one old man, a still-sleepy boy with his books, and "Girlie", their mongrel boat dog. They headed for the docks as fast

133

as the old 15 h.p. Johnson could take them.

The walk to the convent school on Truman Avenue always seemed a pleasant stroll to the father who, at 60, was still erect and muscular. It was more difficult for the boy who struggled to keep up on his shorter legs. By the time they arrived, he was wide awake and had broken a sweat.

Now he just panted as his father performed the same ritual every day. He got down on one knee so he was at eye level to the boy and said, "Do your personal best and be a gentleman." This he followed with a kiss which, even into his young manhood, never embarrassed the boy.

With a respectful, "Yes, sir," the boy wheeled about and did his father's bidding. Nobody ever kidded Little C.B. about where he lived, the kiss, or the name. He was always big for his age and had been taught by his father never to start a fight, but never to run from one.

C.B. McCabe was not only a man of ritual but also of habit. From the school he would make his way to El Cacique on Duval Street where his café con leche and Cuban toast were always waiting. Girlie got the last bite and usually further treats from the waitresses who vied for C.B.'s attention. His reputation was legend. The story of his 1959 Bolita winning of ten thousand dollars and the subsequent Bacchanalian adventure to Cuba with a friend had been told a thousand times on the island. Rum ... Cohibas ... three at a time ... a week ... home ... broke and famous.

C.B. had no time now for remembering and storytelling. He had a boy who needed him and a living to make. He and Girlie took on provisions of water and food and made for the flats off Trumbo Basin for a grueling day of searching for sheepswool sponges in the hot summer sun. He was the last one doing it.

After taking care of some personal business on the playground after school, Little C.B. made his way to his usual haunt down at the city aquarium where he'd hang out with the manager's kids who worked there, the old black man who cleaned the shells in back, or sometimes there was the odd crew of hippies who worked fixing up the buildings.

The boy was always good-natured and even enjoyed the joshing by the men. Sometimes, just for fun, he'd pitch in and do some work or hang out with the workers late in the day as they sat around with their cold beer and talked. But at exactly four forty five, Miss Gracie, the ticket lady at the aquarium, would ring the show bell and call out to him, "C.B.! Time to get on down to the dock."

No matter what he was doing it was over at that moment and he headed to the dock. He knew his father loved him beyond life itself, but he would brook no disobedience and that included tardiness. The penalties for testing his father's resolve were swift, sure and unpleasant. He went for another reason, though, more than anything else. He loved his father in full, measure for measure. C.B. was his hero, his friend and mentor ... of course, first and always, he was his father.

At precisely 5:00 the little johnboat rounded Fleming Key by the Coast Guard base. Little C.B. would hear the putt-putt of the engine just moments before he caught first sight of Girlie in her standard position standing on the bow, eyes intent and immobile like one of the figureheads of the old sailing ships in books that he liked looking at. Little C.B. knew without ever thinking it that he was very lucky. He loved the sea and everything about it. The fish, birds, colors and wind were his world and his father knew just about everything there was to know about life in and on the sea.

At precisely the right moment, C.B. swung the tiller extension mounted on the outboard and cut the power. The little boat coasted into a perfect bow out position and gently bumped the port side into the dock. "Hey, Pa, how was the day?"

"Good, son. Got around four dozen sheepswool. Even managed to get us a grouper for supper. Say, what's that bruise on your cheek?"

"Oh, nothin' I just had a little business after school with that Perez kid."

"I'm not going to hear from the Mother Superior, am I? You know I'll have to whip you, boy."

"No, sir. They might not say so but I think they wanted me to settle his hash. He's a real bully and he messes with the girls when he oughtn't."

"Alright, son, get in."

Little C.B. stepped lightly into the bow and sat down to acknowledge the enthusiastic welcome of Girlie with an ear scratch. He was mightily relieved to be over the fight issue with his father. As big as he was and as much carousing as his father had done, it was ironic that when it came to Little C.B. the father demanded a more pacifistic life for his boy. He was not even allowed to play sports because of his father's fear that, "he might hurt someone." The high school coach of the perennially losing football team was pretty sore about it but wasn't going to argue the point with C.B. His lank, powerful body and bony, weathered hands had leveled meaner men from Cuba to Nassau.

"You know, to be a sponger you got to have a weak nose and a strong stomach," chuckled C.B. as he covered the day's catch with wet burlap so they'd "cure" before the arduous process of spanking out the gurry over and over to yield the soft sponges, "fit for a queen's bath," as he used to say. Little C.B. had heard the quip a thousand times but always managed a dutiful smile and corresponding giggle. What he really was looking forward to was supper.

The years of fishing, conching, sponging and even shrimping a few times had enhanced C.B.'s natural talent as a cook. His recipes for conch soup, breaded turtle, dirty rice, and "smuttered" fish were legend and enough to get him invited to any gathering of men or the bed of almost any woman.

"Well, what say you boy? What shall we do with this fine fellow?" he said as he deftly gutted and filleted the Nassau grouper.

"Gotta keep this backbone son. You know that's the secret of boiled fish soup. Lets the natural oils out and makes it taste like butter. Put it in the ice box, son, and I'll cook it up in the morning for breakfast."

"Sure, Pa. Say, if it's okay, how 'bout frying the fish? Thata way Girlie can have some hush puppies."

"Thata? What kind of word is thata? You know I never got beyond eighth grade. It's no sin to be poor like us, but it is a sin to look and act poor."

"I'm sorry, Pa," the boy said, ashamedly. Worse than

anything in the world he hated to disappoint his father.

After dinner while C.B. sat and smoked in the cockpit, Little C.B. washed the few dishes and put them up. He would remember these meals for their elegant simplicity. The freshest seafood with a few spices done in perfect harmony. Two pots, two plates, two bowls, two forks, two cups. The lesson of 'less is more' was repeated to the point it would be ingrained forever in everything the boy did.

"There she goes," mused C.B. Little C.B. instinctively turned his eyes west just in time to catch the last sliver of the sun as it melted like a glob of yellow butter into the horizon.

"Now you know if'n you ever see a flash of green you can make a wish and it'll come true."

"Yes sir, Pa. I remember. Did you ever see it happen?"

"Son, I've seen everything there is to see on these waters. Yeah, hell, I saw it! Made my wish and bang, just like that, the next day my number hit and I won ten grand. Let me tell you that was a whole pile of money back then. But, boy, in this life be careful what you wish for. You just might get it."

"What's bad about winning a whole bunch of money, Pa?"

"Well, I'll tell you. Gittin' a wish makes you plumb stupid. Anything you don't get with an honest day's labor, well, you just don't appreciate it."

"Boy, I'd like to have ten grand," said the boy trying out the words.

"Yeah? Is that what you'd wish for?"

"Oh no, I just meant it'd be nice to have ten grand. Heck, I'd buy you a better johnboat, a collar for Girlie and a pocket knife."

C.B. chuckled. "Yeah. That'd be nice. What would you wish for, son?" Without hesitation Little C.B. answered, "I'd wish we'd always live like this and some day I'd be just like you and know all there is to know about the ocean and fishing."

"That makes me real proud, son," he said, turning his head so his son wouldn't see him misting up. He quickly changed the subject. "Now there's old Venus right on time."

Little C.B. again turned to the west to see the bright, steady light of the emerging planet.

"Now, how do you know a star from a planet?"

"Planets reflect light so they don't twinkle."

"That's right, boy. And what's the most important star?"

"The North Star, Polaris, because the whole universe rotates around it so it never moves and you can always know where to steer."

"Good boy."

The ritual of teaching, showing and testing was constant in their lives. C.B. loved to share his knowledge and the boy absorbed it like a fine sponge.

The night fell over them like a blanket falling in slow motion. The memory of a whoosh of air as his mother, long ago, spread the sheet over him was somewhere in the sensation of nightfall as stars came out like diamonds being thrown across the universe by an invisible hand. There was no cloud or moon and a gentle breeze rocked the boat to the slap of water on the hull. Soon the boy was sound asleep, cozily wrapped in the old quilt from his bed with Girlie pressed close for their mutual warmth and safety.

"Good morning, son," said the father cheerily. "The fish and grits is done. How do you want your eggs?"

"Over, Pa, and good morning to you." He yawned as Girlie moved off the blanket. "I fell asleep I guess, huh?" he said a little sheepishly.

"Yep, you looked so whipped and the night being so nice and all, I just let you be."

"Thanks, Pa," he said as he stood at the stern unzipping his pants to relieve the ache in his belly over the side.

"We're just two kings, aren't we boy?" C.B. sighed loudly after the big breakfast of eggs, boiled fish, grits and biscuits.

Leaning back contentedly, "It just doesn't git any better."

"Sure doesn't, Pa. Say, after I do the dishes, what are we going to do today?"

"Well, Mr. Thompson told me he'd like a couple new sharks for the aquarium so I thought we'd head up toward Ballast Key flats and see what we can do."

"Yippee," the boy offered excitedly. There was nothing he liked better than hunting sharks. The danger and skill touched something deep inside and made his gut feel funny.

"What kind of sharks, Pa?"

"Well, at least a nurse shark, maybe a black tip. Anyway the tide will be just about right in two hours so we better get going. You know we gotta get 'em back here quick so they don't die."

"I'll get the dishes done super fast, Pa!"

"Alright, son, I'll git the rigs made up and we'll shove off."

"Over there. See 'em?"

Little C.B. strained to see what his father was pointing to. It was always this way. C.B. navigated by landmarks infallibly finding the exact place whether it was for fish, sharks, conch or sponges. He had no depth gauge, Loran or GPS. He didn't even wear sunglasses. His gaze under the tattered straw hat could tell the depth and bottom from so far away even practiced fishermen couldn't understand how he did it.

"See the birds diving? They're picking up scraps and smaller fish around the feeding. I'm going to cut the engine and we'll drift right to it."

Sure enough, C.B. had maneuvered perfectly upwind of the sharks feeding on the incoming tide and they slowly glided toward the churning water.

"Alright, boy, git ready. They usually don't spook right away but with sharks you just never know."

Little C.B. could feel his palms start to sweat and the prickles stand up on the back of his neck. Girlie was as immobile as stone staring intently from the bow.

"OK, boy," his father whispered. "Drop 'em in."

With that, the lines went in. They were heavy, green cord rigged with steel leaders and huge stainless 12/0 hooks disguised in fish heads.

Now Little C.B. couldn't help but see. They were right on top of the swirling mass of ten to twelve nurse sharks just twelve feet below. He watched with glorious anticipation as his bait drifted down. The first shark came up on it and Little C.B. hoped he wouldn't take it because he was a large bull and he knew he was too big to bring in. Luckily, the bull moved away. The boy had a thought it was from experience. Just then a five foot nurse glided over and the bait disappeared. The sweat was pouring out and stung his eyes. At first it was a steady pulling away and then the frantic jerking of fear that pulled the line taut and into the flesh of his fingers.

"I got 'im! I got 'im!" he heard himself scream.

"Steady boy. Set the hook, then hand over hand. Don't let it go slack. Bring him in quick so he don't kill himself in the fight."

Little C.B. knew his father would only advise but wouldn't help him pull the shark in. It was C.B's way. If you were man enough to start something you'd better be man enough to finish it.

A five foot shark will go about fifty pounds. Add to that every muscle in the shark resisting and the dead lift from the bottom with no reel or pole and you've got a man's work.

Little C.B. was now straining with everything he had. Sweat had already soaked his shirt and the veins were bulging to the surface of his reddening face.

"He's heavy, Pa!" he managed to gasp out.

"Yep, he's gonna be tough. Just hold him a while so's he tires out some. Don't worry about the line. It won't break and he can't bite through the steel leader. You got 'im good boy. Just hang on."

Little C.B. could feel more than see the shark going first left then right, snapping his broad head back and forth trying to shake the unseen, unfamiliar hook painfully lodged in the roof of his mouth. The thick green cord was buried in his fingers in a reverse hand over hand position his father had taught him that gave him maximum leverage but still felt like it was going to clip his fingers off at the first knuckle. He had a sense of envy for the leather tough skin on his father's hands that could be gentle or punishing but never soft.

Instinctively, Little C.B. dropped the line on the wooden gunnel of the boat to transfer the pull that seemed would never abate. Just then the shark lurched and brought the boy's hands hard into the side of the boat, breaking the skin on his knuckles and, at the same time, slicing the cord neat as a razor through the creases of his fingers.

"Eee!!" he cried while automatically tightening his grip and pulling back and down on the line against the gunnel. It was a reflex action against the brain's demand to let go, to get away from cuts now stinging with salt.

C.B. saw immediately the blood starting to drip through his son's palms onto the deck.

"Let 'im go, boy! He's too big."

"Like hell I will!" shrilled the boy uncharacteristically. "I got 'im and that's that."

"Alright. Just let 'im wear down then. That last pull took a lot out of him. Maybe he'll give up first."

Little C.B. was able to hold the stalemate for another five minutes until the shark stopped pulling and jerking.

"Alright, son, he's tired and resting. Time to bring 'im up."

The boy stood, lifting the line off the gunnel, and immediately started the slow hand over hand lift of the still bulk of the shark.

"Is he dead, Pa?"

The answer came not from the father but the shark as it jerked its head half heartedly.

"No, boy. You just plumb tuckered him out. Sharks get that way pretty quick. Just keep the line taut and bring him up."

Ignoring the excruciating pain of his bleeding fingers that the fresh salt water only made worse, he pulled one arm length and then the next until the shark was along side the boat.

"Hold steady boy."

Without another word, C.B. positioned himself at about the middle of the shark, reached under him behind the mouth and, at the same time, grabbed the tail. The shark made a few futile thrashing swings but it was over and C.B. deftly, almost gently, picked him over the gunnel and into the six foot live well in one sure move.

"Yew! You did it boy! He's a beauty."

A grin spread over the exhausted boy's face as he leaned over to get a better look at his take.

"I did, didn't I, Pa?"

"You sure did, son, and he's every bit of five feet. Hell, most men would've cut him loose. I'm proud of you boy!"

The whoops and cries that always accompanied their big takes died down. "Lemme see those hands, son. They look pretty tore up."

"I'm alright, Pa. It was worth it," he said as he painfully uncurled his hands palm up.

The old man shook his head in silence, reached into the seat compartment of the boat that served as dry storage, and took out an old battered army surplus medical kit.

"This is going to burn like all hell, son. I'm sorry. These cuts are plenty deep."

"I know, Pa. Go on ahead. I'm OK."

As the old man poured the Mercurochrome over his son's palms, the boy felt like he'd thrust his hands into a coal fire, but he bit his lip and strained not to yelp.

"Go ahead and yell if you want to. Ain't no one here but me and your shark."

"No, I'll not yell, Pa," the boy managed with no little effort.

"There, that's good. I'll wrap you up and we'll get outta here. After all this, we want to get this here big fellow to Mr. Thompson so's we get paid. Right son?"

"Yes sir, Pa. We sure don't want him dying on us."

The father hesitated a moment then looked his boy in the eye and put a hand on his shoulder and said, "You done good, son. You got grit and stick-to-it-ness. I'm proud of you."

"Sometimes a man's got to do what a man's got to," said the boy returning an earnest look into his father's eyes.

The old man just smiled.

TRUE NORTH

Bong! Bong! Bong! The new XJ8 Jaguar open door alarm made the softer version of the department store paging bells Jack Snyder remembered as a boy when he went into the big city with his mother. A lot had changed in his life since then, including what he used to think was important.

It's funny how noises and smells can take you back in time, he thought as he settled back into the rich leather seats that made a satisfying crunch under his weight.

I remember my first car was a second hand 1962 MGB. I paid $850 for it and spent the whole summer before my sophomore year at Penn fixing it up. New top, reworked engine, paint, tires, stereo, exhaust system, even a walnut gear shift knob and steering wheel. God I loved that car. Used to tool through Fairmont Park going through the gears, down shifting on the curves. I remember looking out my apartment window just to see it sitting there waiting for me. There really is some man machine thing.

When I sold it at a profit I felt a hollow sick feeling like the betrayal of a friend. Look at me now. Sitting in a new Jag that cost seventy times what the MG cost and it sure doesn't feel seventy times better. It's clean, quiet, hi tech and ... not me. I could be sitting in a fucking Cadillac for that matter. I'd trade this piece of crap in a minute for that MG. So what's the point of all this?

He was barely aware that he was entering through the

big wrought iron gates on to the brown gravel driveway leading up to his house. It was, of course, in the right part of Main Line Philadelphia.

An older house of stone, it was built by a banker who had blown his brains out in the '29 crash. It had been continually occupied since then by various business types, scions of society and doctors, a general stream of unnoticed people whose sole connection was the passing of money and brief stewardship of the place. The matured trees gave it a coveted sense of isolation and attested to the continuum of a benign investment in gardeners.

It was a big house, not huge, but certainly big. Six bedrooms, eight baths, various salons, a game room, detached servants quarters, four-car garage, a pool and tennis court used only when the kids came home from school. It was big alright, too big for Jack Snyder and Barbara, his wife of 20 years, and, besides the help, the only permanent residents of the place.

Christ, every time I drive up to this place my stomach gets cold. After Penn and Harvard get their extortion money, Barbara's folks are taken care of at that country club retirement home in Vero Beach, the mortgage on this place picks the meat off my bones. What in God's name was I thinking when I let her talk me into this place. What'd she call it? Our station in life? A necessary tool for entertaining? Jeezus, I must have 'STUPID' written on my forehead. The happiest I've ever been was that first fixer upper townhouse we bought in Society Hill in the 70's. It was small but seemed like a palace at the time. Whoever said bigger is better? Bigger is just bigger. I gotta sell this barn. Sure I do.

"Hi, how was your day?" his wife said distractedly from the couch barely, looking up from the recent issue of *Palm Beach Life* magazine she was reading.

"Do you want a drink?" she asked.

"Do bears crap in the woods?" Jack replied.

"I wish you wouldn't talk like that."

"Why, who are we trying to impress with our station in life today?"

"Jack, let's not fight shall we? And anyway I wish you wouldn't drink. I'd like to talk to you tonight about mom and dad."

"Oh swell. How much is this going to cost me?"

"Damn you, they are the grandparents to your children!"

"Well, I'm gonna have a drink anyway. You want anything?"

"No. You'd better make it a double. You're late and dinner's almost ready."

"I was gonna make it a double and I'm not ready to eat."

"Jack, you really are a selfish bastard. How easy do you think it is to get a good cook like Conchita? She'll leave if she's not appreciated you know."

"Appreciated? Christ Barbara! Listen to yourself. She's help, a cook, a hired servant. She's not my mother. She does work, she gets paid. Value for value. Quid pro quo. Appreciated? I'm polite and my checks don't bounce and god dammit if I wanna eat at seven instead of six thirty, I'm gonna eat at goddam seven."

"Then you'll be dining alone. I'll make your apologies and have Conchita put your dinner in the fridge.

As Barbara exited the den Jack had the sensation of releasing a breath of held air. Not having to continue conversation with her was a relief he hated but sought by being rude or coarse to her.

Appreciated? Make apologies? Fridge? Christ, she's changed, he thought morosely as he fell into the overstuffed club chair he favored.

She's as common as I am ... common as dirt. Where does she come off with this crap. This sense of superiority and Muffy and Biff, old money, prep school, Harvard society slang. *Fridge* ... it's a refrigerator goddamit. Yeah, I went to Penn, did well and made a bucket of money. That doesn't change who I am and certainly not her! Money doesn't change you except to make you responsible for more stuff and people than you need. Maybe it does change the way you want people to think about you. What's the urge in humans to need affirmation and approval from complete strangers. When you get right down to it, we're no different from dogs smelling each other's butts and either rolling over on our backs and wetting ourselves or making the other guy do it.

God, at one time she was beautiful, though. Not just pretty, but beautiful through her entire being, so beautiful that it just had to radiate out of her eyes and with a smile that could light up a room. She never used to use perfume but always smelled sweet and cool. I remember how soft her hair was, and how I practically came just to look at her naked body at our secret picnic spot, lying back on a blanket, her arms held up to me with the sun turning her white, unblemished skin into a surreal vision of innocent desire. Her soft moaning, her rock hard nipples, the velveteen triangle of hair ... good God, what's happened?" he thought with a shudder like the one you get when you feel a fearful unknown presence behind you.

We haven't slept together in six months. I snore and sleep in the guest room. She smells funny to me and when I see her stained panties on the bathroom floor I get nauseous.

Jack had typically brought home a brief case stuffed with reports but just as typically these days after three double bourbons and water, he was fast asleep in the embrace of the overstuffed club chair. That was where he found himself the next morning, feeling seedy and slightly sick with a headache and a briefcase full of unread reports.

On arrival at his office he was met by Mrs. Tully and her indefatigable cheer. "Good morning, Mr. Snyder. You don't look well. Are you alright?"

"Yeah, I just stayed up too late reading reports," Jack lied.

"Mr. Snyder you shouldn't work so hard. It's not good for you."

"Yeah, you're probably right. It just seems like there's not enough time. Any messages?"

"Not yet. But don't forget you have a meeting with Mr. Bradford at ten."

Jack's stomach tightened as he thought to himself, Jesus, how could I forget. Today's the day when I have to report to Bradford on the merger. Shit! Shit! Shit! My ass is in a sling now. I'm not prepared. As dumb as he is, I don't even have enough to bullshit him.

"Get me some coffee," Jack snapped as he went into his office with his panic.

151

"Yes s...," said a puzzled Mrs. Tully to the door as it slammed shut.

Well, boy, now you've done it. Five mill of commissions on the line and you can't seem to get with the program. What kind of schmuck are you? You're the golden boy, the wunderkind, youngest guy to make partner. You're a putz, a procrastinating lazy drunk who hides it all too well. I hate this job!

A soft knock heralded the arrival of a tentative Mrs. Tully with his coffee. "Here's our coffee," she tried meekly.

"Sorry I snapped at you. You're right, I am working too hard. Get Bradford on the line will you please?"

"Of course, sir, right away!" Mrs. Tully retreated with downcast eyes.

Add prick to the list, he thought to himself as the door closed without making a sound.

"Mr. Snyder, Mr. Bradford's on the line," came Mrs. Tully's voice over the intercom.

"Thanks," he said as he stabbed the blinking button with his finger.

"Charlie," he said with as much cheer and old-boy enthusiasm as he could muster. "How ya doing pal?"

"Well I guess I'm alright. But I didn't sleep well last night. You know this deal is far from done. Those Hebes over at Goldman are still sniffing around."

Jack winced. He had gone to Wharton and made life long friends there, many of whom were Jewish. He was even one of the few *'goy boys'* they let into the Sigma Alpha Mu house. At the time it was one of the best houses full of rich Jewish jocks. This association was recognized but politely never mentioned around Bradford, Whitney and Aitherwaite.

Charlie Bradford was the book smart, street dumb heir of 'Big' Bill Bradford, the legendary and brilliant founder of one of Philadelphia's most successful private banks that catered to the crème de la crème of old Philly money. Charlie was an arrogant, country club regular whose prejudices and obvious difference from 'Big Bill' made him a nervous object of ridicule amongst colleagues, contemporaries and friends alike. Big Bill must have felt like he was throwing a 'Hail Mary' when he left control of the firm to Charlie, the only issue of his marriage and subsequently the anointed heir de rigueur of the great man.

"Charlie, what are you worried about? Both parties want it to happen, the letter of intent is clean, the due diligence is almost done with no big surprises and besides, you've got your best man on it ... me." Jack forced a sip of hot coffee to wet a mouth suddenly gone dry. He knew what was going to happen next.

"What do you mean, almost done? Today's the day, Jack. You're supposed to deliver the report today. Remember? May 3, 5:00 pm? We're talking about a hundred million dollar deal here. Five million in commissions, stock warrants, captive accounts, a piece of the insurance, maybe some spin off benefits! It could be worth ten mill! Am I clear?"

"Take it easy Charlie. Don't I always come through? Look these guys want it so bad I'm not going to have a problem getting an extra two days. Besides, I want to take another look at the Baltimore plant."

"Again? Christ, what for? We've been there three times

and ..."

"Yeah, but always with them and at their invitation. Look, I'm sure everything's okay but there may be a possibility the inventories aren't what they say and you know, if we sign off and they're not right, Bradford & Whitney is fucked."

After a silence, Bradford's meek voice came back over the line. "Are you sure?"

"Hell no! But what is it you always tell me, *First integrity then profitability*," boomed Jack with the assurance of knowing he was getting a reprieve. "Do you really want to take the chance?"

"No, 'integrity first'. That's what dad always said. Alright, get down to Baltimore and take a look. Oh, you'll need to get the extension first, you know."

"Yeah, yeah, don't worry I know what to do."

When Jack put the phone back on the cradle he watched his hand like it was detached from his body. It was shaking violently and his shirt was soaked with sweat.

"The new Jag oozed along the highway to the marina in exactly the opposite direction from Baltimore. Jack didn't need to see the inventory. He'd checked it out and had bonded certificates and he knew it. He'd ginned up some excuse and both parties had bought it. If nothing else, he was one hell of a salesman. He just needed to clear his head and do the math.

At least I still have some shred of professional pride left, he thought to himself as he made his way to where his beloved *Mikko* was snugly tied to the dock of his private boat house.

She was nothing short of exquisite even though she

154

was built in the thirties. *Mikko* was one of the last sharpies built by Ralph Munroe in Coconut Grove, Florida where Jack grew up on stories of the legendary pioneer boat builder. Buying her and restoring her at a cost of $150,000 was the thing of which Jack was most proud in his life. She was twenty four feet of handcrafted beauty made with wood that could no longer be bought at any price. Under his skillful hand she responded like a well trained thoroughbred and down wind nothing could touch her. If Jack had a love affair in life it was with *Mikko*.

After removing her cover as carefully as you'd remove a bride's dress on the first night, Jack stood in the neat little cockpit and looked her over without regard to time or circumstance, just his passion for the little craft.

Yeah, this is what I needed, he thought as he hopped up onto the dock making the *Mikko* slap in the water causing a noise that Jack thought sounded like, 'Let's go, let's go, let's go.'

"I'll be right back, darlin'," he said aloud as he went up to the boat house door. He had the static-shock surprise like when you touch an elevator button in the winter as the key slid into the hole and he heard the phone ring inside at the same moment.

"Dammit! Now what the hell is that?"

He picked up the phone to hear the monotonous voice of his message forwarding service.

"You have one unheard message. Message one ..."

"Jack! Jack! Where are you, goddammit?" All hell's broken loose! Those bastards at Goldmans got wind that we aren't closing and slipped in a verbal offer and shit, they're thinking about it! Fuck, I knew this could happen!

You goddamn call me, you hear me?" The sheer panic made Charlie's voice go up in pitch until he was squealing like a pig with a slit throat. Jack didn't know whether to laugh or cry. He chuckled then started to laugh hysterically as tears poured out of his closed eyes. All the pent up anger, frustrations, fear and disillusionment kept in check for so long welled up and spilled over the edge of his sanity. Alternately, he laughed until he couldn't breathe then cried until no tears were left. Time lost all meaning until he became aware that it was getting dark in the rough but neat little cabin in which he felt more safe and comfortable than anywhere on earth. He seemed to awaken from a refreshingly long nap and knew with more purpose than he could ever remember what he was going to do. He picked up the phone and dialed Charles Bradford II at Bradford, Whitney & Aitherwaite.

"Hello, Beth," he heard himself say to the familiar voice of Charlie's long-suffering secretary.

"I'll put you right through Mr. Snyder," she said without the usual pleasantries.

"Thank God! Jack, where are you?" Charlie gasped almost like he was going to expire on the spot.

"I'm at the boat house," Jack responded in a cool voice that surprised even him.

"Wh ... what did you say?" Charlie stuttered after a stunned silence.

"You heard me old pal. I'm at the boat house."

"You're not in Baltimore?"

"That shithole? What for?"

"The deal you fucking idiot. The deal. You were supposed to be checking out the inventories or something.

What are you doing at your goddammed boat house?" he exploded.

"Well, I thought I'd go sailing actually."

"Have you lost your fucking mind? If we lose this deal I'm holding you directly responsible. I'll break your back! Do you understand what I'm saying, Jack?"

"Sure Charlie. I know exactly what you're saying. Let me save you the trouble. If the deal goes south I'll take the responsibility. It'll be my fault, okay? You can tell everybody at the club I screwed up and how I'll never work in this '*bidness*' again," he said parodying Charlie's frequent Jew baiting.

"But you know ... I ain't gonna work in this business again anyway so I really don't give a shit. Charlie, it's a good deal and the inventories are fine. Just wrap it up."

"But ... but I can't," he sputtered. "You ... "

"That may be true Charlie. You really aren't very good at all this, are you? You're a rich man Charlie. Why don't you hang it up and go garden or paint or something. You're never going to be 'Big Charlie' you now."

"You fucking ass ... " the dial tone cut him off as Jack hung up the phone. As he walked down the dock to *Mikko*, he heard the phone ringing until it finally stopped. As he sat in *Mikko's* cabin looking at the charts that would take him down the coast to Key West, he noted the couple of degrees difference in the chart reference and his compass and thought to himself, "Yea, from now on Jackie my boy, use other people's charts but steer true north with your own compass.

CAREFUL WHAT YOU WISH FOR

Jefferson Spath was a malcontent. If there was ever anyone who embodied the meaning of the word it was he. On the most beautiful day of spring he would long for the snows of winter. If he was at the theater - a rare event because he was never satisfied with what was playing - he would be hungry for dinner. If he was, on even rarer occasions, with one woman, he would find himself pining for another. This condition of his existence never seemed to bother him though it drove mad anyone unlucky enough to be in his company. The words "insufferable", "boor", "rude", and "indecisive" rolled off the mantle of his persona with never a thought. For Jefferson Spath the grass was truly always greener somewhere else. All this would soon change.

Spath lived alone on the third floor of his apartment building though he desperately wanted to be on the fourth and top floor, a desire he never failed to mention to the occupant, one Delphos Goldman.

Goldman also lived alone and rarely ventured out during the day having most necessities delivered. The deliveries were always from the best purveyors, a fact which did not escape the jealous eye of Jefferson Spath. His food came from Dean and DeLucca's. His clothes were sent from an unfamiliar address in London. Fresh flowers appeared every day at precisely 10:00 am.

Spath hated him. Spath hated him for his name, for what kind of name is Delphos? He hated him for his apparent wealth. Mostly, he hated him because he wanted his apartment.

"Good morning, Mr. Goldman and how are you today?" Spath dripped in greeting this particular morning.

"Good morning, Mr. Spath," replied the elderly gentleman with a hint of resignation that his attempt at avoiding his neighbor was unsuccessful.

"I'm well and you?" Goldman heard himself answering against his will but in compliance with some social code of his nature.

"Well, actually, I'd be a lot better if I was on the top floor like you. Ha! Ha! Yeah, I bet it's a lot quieter up there. You wouldn't be thinking of giving up that place any time soon would you?"

"No Mr. Spath for the thousandth time, I'm very content and have no plans to give up ... my home."

"Oh, well I guess it never hurts to ask and I've told you a million times, don't exaggerate. Ha! Ha!"

Goldman started to turn toward the elevator, paused, then turned to face Jefferson Spath.

"No, actually it has been a thousand times. Exactly a thousand. You've been asking me this same ignorant question from the day you moved in."

"No, I haven't. That's not true."

"Oh, but I assure you it is true. I know you Jefferson Spath. I've listened to you tell me about your stupid boss, about the women foolish enough to go out with you on a first, never to be repeated, date. You complain about the weather spring, summer, fall and winter. You don't like the president, the governor or the mayor. In fact, I don't believe, and let me be careful here, no I don't believe I've ever heard you say that anything, anywhere, at any time has ever suited you."

"Now, see here, I was just making pleasant conversation. You don't have to . . ."

"Pleasant? Sir, I don't think you appreciate the word. You are singularly the most wretched man I've come into contact with in the past two hundred years. I . . .," he stopped abruptly when he realized he'd gone too far.

"Two hundred years? What's that supposed to mean?"

"Nothing. Forget I said it. I'm sorry for what I said."

The two men stood for a moment of embarrassed silence. One didn't know what to say. The other knew he had said too much and knew he must rectify a serious faux pas. The curtain of his anonymity had been lifted and with a Jefferson Spath he had to do something. He thought, then broke their silence.

"Look Jefferson, I obviously am a bit rattled. I mean two hundred years! Ha! I wonder where that came from. Look, why don't you come up to my place for a glass of port?"

"Well, that's better. Sure, I guess that would be fine. I mean, we're neighbors, aren't we? Ha! Ha!"

"Yes, that we are. Do come in an hour. In fact, I have something for you. A present, if you will."

At the appointed time, Jefferson Spath touched the button of the elevator while his mind was spinning. He had never been to Goldman's. In fact, in five years he couldn't remember anyone actually going inside

Goldman's. At once he was afraid and in a state of high excitement. For once he really was looking forward to something. His knock on the door was met almost immediately by Goldman in an elegant smoking jacket, flannel pants and soft leather slippers, all of obvious high quality, but looking a bit Victorian in style.

"Oh good. Right on time. May I call you Jefferson?"

"Why yes, of course, and may I return the compliment by calling you Delphos?"

"You may, but my friends call me Del."

Spath was momentarily off balance. Del? He had friends?

"Alright then, Del it is."

As Goldman led the way, Spath couldn't help noticing the lavish and obviously expensive décor of the apartment. Fine oriental carpets, heavy leather furniture, artworks that had to be copies. Didn't they? There were books everywhere. Fine leather-bound books with titles that spun by his view in a profusion of familiarity: Dante, Twain, Voltaire, Socrates, Shakespeare.

"Have you read all these?" was all Spath could manage.

"Oh, yes, several times. Right this way to my study."

Goldman showed Spath the way off a spacious living room to a smaller room that at once felt secure, and unmistakably, a pleasant place to be. It, too, was surrounded by shelves of books as well as a wall of musical instruments - a cello, violin, clarinet, recorder and even an Irish tin pipe.

"Sit here, Jefferson," said Goldman motioning the somewhat awestruck younger man to one of the two

English club chairs. "May I pour you a glass of port?"

"Why yes, of course."

"It's a very good '48 directly from the Duoro in Portugal. I've opened and decanted it in honor of your visit."

After a toast, which Goldman offered in Latin, Jefferson put the glass to his lips to taste the most elegant and complex drink of his life.

"What was that you said?"

"*Nihil tibi a me postulanti recusabo?* It means I will refuse you nothing."

"Really, what an odd toast. Why would you say that?"

"Because, my new found friend, I am compelled by my outburst downstairs to be interested in you and to help you."

"And why must you help me, not that I feel I need any particular help?"

"Because you do. You most certainly do. I'll prove it to you. Name something you are content with at this moment. Your apartment? No, that's what started all this. Your social life? Do you have one? Your work? You make good money but you call it work with an undeniable emphasis on the word. No, Jefferson, you're not a happy fellow and I can help you. Here, have another glass."

"Alright, let's just say I need help. How can you help me?"

"Many ways, but you must at least know what you think would make you happy and be careful what you wish for.

"Well, money, of course," Spath said almost instantaneously.

"Ah, I might have guessed but, just for the sake of asking, why would money make you happy?"

"Oh, come now. Let's not be naïve. What is it that money can't do? It can change where you live, everything about how you live and I don't care what anyone says, with enough money any woman can be yours. Say, may I have a tad more of that port, it's quite good."

"Yes, of course. Well, money it shall be then. Whether I agree with you or not, *fide data et accepter*, if that's what you want then I shall oblige."

"So what, you gonna give me some dough?" asked Spath who was more than a little elevated by the port Goldman kept pouring into his more-often-than not-empty glass.

"Not exactly, but I'll give you the means to your desire."

"Okay, shure," Spath slurred out.

"On two conditions. You can never ask where I got it or tell anyone you have it and you must never talk to me again."

"All right," Spath said through a silly grin that allowed a small trickle of spittle to escape the corner of his mouth. "That's not being a pal, but okay."

"Here," said Goldman handing Spath a *New York Times* newspaper.

"Oh, geez Del, I can't really accept this. I mean hell, you opened a 1984 .."

"1948."

"Yeah, a 1948 bottle of really good juice. I can't take your paper. How you gonna know what's on TV tonight?"

"Look closer."

"Huh, okay, lessee, New York Times. Yep, it's a newspaper all right."

"Look closer."

"OK, whassis say? Vol. 936 May 3, 2006. Hey, I'm a little tooted but this is May 2nd. I know that for sure. Whas this some kinda trick? Say, can I have just one more li'l slurp of that port?"

"I think you'll find the paper is exactly accurate to what's going to happen ... tomorrow."

"Ah, come on. Excuse me, but that's bullshit. Nope, not possible."

"I said I'd refuse you nothing and I've not. You've asked for money and I've given you the means. What you do is up to you. And now, Jefferson," Goldman said standing up, I must bid you good day. I'm working on some things and need to get back to them."

Spath blinked and rose a little unsteadily and said, "Okay, swell. Thanks for the port and the uh ... present. Can't wait to read it."

"Oh, you'll find it quite interesting I assure you."

Later, back in his own less extravagantly appointed apartment Spath sat down heavily on the couch next to where he had thrown the newspaper Goldman have given to him. For a while he just sat in the early evening light and stared dumbly at the blank TV screen. He started to reach for the remote but, since it was under the paper, he was obliged to pick it up saying to himself, "Oh, what the hell."

He looked at the paper grinning stupidly and said, "Alright, let's just see," and opened it to the lottery numbers for this evening's drawing. To his complete befuddlement there it was, results for May 3, 2006: 3-27-33-42-48-58. Estimated Jackpot $20 million. He rubbed his eyes, got up, went to the kitchen and checked the calendar stuck on the cork bulletin board.

"What the ... May 2. What's my watch say, 2. What's going on? That bastard's playing with me!"

His call to the date and time line confirmed that it was indeed 6:30 pm, May 2, 2006.

"Alright, this is crazy and I'm drunk but I'm gonna go get a damned lottery ticket."

With no little effort, for he was feeling a little queasy, he went down the block to the Korean grocery store and bought lottery ticket number 3-27-33-42-48-58.

"Good luck. You gimme 10% you win?" the Korean smiled at Spath.

"Yeah, sure, whatever."

He didn't make it home before vomiting a purplish ooze that only made him sicker. He was asleep before his head hit the pillow.

The change in street noise always woke him at 6:00 and today was no exception but for the violent headache that had been throbbing for the previous hour.

Spath's morning rituals didn't vary until he remembered the previous evening and the lottery ticket. He rushed through his shower, dressed hurriedly and ran to the grocery store where he was greeted by the Korean shouting "You win! You win! Lottery ticket you buy last night win!"

Spath pulled the ticket from his pocket and with trembling finger straightened it to see the numbers.

"3-27-33-42-48-58," he read on the scrolling light sign

on the back of the ticket printer.

"Holy Mother of God, I won! I won!"

"You give me one million like you say," said the Korean.

"Fuck off, Ho Chi," said Spath over his shoulder as he burst through the door to the street. He couldn't believe this was happening but he knew exactly what he was going to do next.

The continual beating on the fourth floor apartment finally brought an irritated Goldman.

"What do you want? I told you never to talk to me again."

"Are you out of your mind? I won! I played the lottery number in that trick paper of yours and I won!"

"So? I told you I'd give you the means to get what you wanted now live up to your word and leave me alone," he said. As he tried to shut the door, Spath put his foot in the way and pushed it back open.

"Not so fast. I wanna know how you did that."

"That's the second part of your word you're breaking. I told you not to ask me that."

"I don't care. All bets are off, you crazy bastard. You tell me right now or I'm going to tell the newspapers about how I won when I pick up my check, and guess what? Your life here is over. I'll even get your apartment."

"*O facinus indignum.* Have you no sense of dignity? You didn't even bother to say thank you!"

"Yeah, well I figure there's plenty more where this came from. What's it going to be, Del?"

Goldman sagged into a hall chair and said, "Alright, what is it you want?"

167

"Now that's more like it. I want to know how you did it."

"I can't tell you."

"I'm warning you, Del."

"No, really, I can't tell you because I don't know."

"Don't B.S. me. What's the deal?"

"I can get the papers only a day at a time from ae society to which I belong and that's all I can say," he said wearily. "Believe me, it's a curse I've lived with for a long time."

"Yeah, well, let me share the burden. We'll see. I want tomorrow's paper .. now!"

"Over there," Goldman nodded to the hall stand where a neatly folded paper was.

"Now we're talking," Spath exclaimed as he rushed over to pick it up.

"*New York Times* May 4, 2006, I can't believe this! Goldie, you're a prince. See, now I'm happy! You did help me! Ha! Ha!"

Goldman's face was sad and he wouldn't look Spath in the eye.

"Come on, old pal. Don't be sad. This is the beginning of a great relationship."

"We'll see. You have what you want now please just go."

"Alright, Goldie, I've got a lot of work to do anyway. You just rest up and get the next paper for me and everything will be fine. See you tomorrow."

As he left, Spath didn't see the hint of a sardonic smile form on Goldman's mouth.

Cashing the lottery ticket took longer than Spath had

hoped. They wanted pictures, background, a story. When he finally got to his new suite at the Waldorf it was already 2:00 pm. He'd have to work fast. He opened several accounts with offshore gaming houses and played every trifecta at every track. He went long on two million dollars of margined stock, one million in options and another million in highly leveraged commodity trades. By his reckoning, his profits by tomorrow would eclipse the lottery winnings by two.

At five o'clock he fell exhausted on to the king sized bed and started laughing deliriously between singing, "I'm in the money da, da, da, da, daa!"

Suddenly he stopped and sat up ramrod stiff.

"What if this is a hoax? What if the lottery was a joke that backfired on Goldman? Just dumb luck! I didn't read the rest of the paper. Hell, he's rich enough to pull of something like a fake paper. What if he counted on me just reading what was obvious? What if all the stuff I just bet on is false? I'll be ruined! The margin calls alone will be over twenty million dollars! That bastard! I'll kill him!" He grabbed his coat, tucked the paper under his arm and ran out of the hotel on his way to Goldman's. He never saw the cab coming around the corner with the Pakistani driver turned in his seat arguing with a passenger. It killed him instantly.

As the crowd gathered around the broken body of the man lying in the street, newspapers were caught in the wind and blown like oversized confetti down the street. One page momentarily slapped against a trash can. If anyone had picked it up and read it, they would have read tomorrow's obituary headline: "Tragedy Strikes Lotto Winner!"

A GOOD MAN

"Well, *Signor Dottore*, here are the keys!" Aldo Rossini's face was lit up in joyful anticipation of his impending commission for acting as the '*immobilieri*' for the purchase of our new farm in Tuscany near Asciano. As a rule, I generally have a distaste - as well as a distrust - for people who make their way not by creating anything, but rather by arranging for others to do so. I quietly hoped he might use some of his new-found wealth to buy some new shirts instead of the frayed-sleeved, sweat-stained one from which protruded the hand holding the keys to our new place.

"Thanks," I said, inwardly hoping he wasn't going to offer the other hand which was usually passing through thin, greasy hair which failed to cover his sweating pate. No such luck there. He grasped and shook my hand with unctuous vigor and then went for my wife whose wincing face left no doubt about her feelings for *Signor* Rossini. I knew Rossini, whose own wife was queen of the myriad crow-like black "nonas" (those whose mustachioed upper lips never turned up in a smile, at least for Americans) would take any opportunity to press against my wife's breasts. I knew I'd hear about it again later.

It was done! Five years of coming and going to this beautiful place, falling in love with the food, the wine and the people, going to night school to learn Italian, and finally making the big break by actually closing my practice and moving to this Tuscan province of Italy.

Whether out of true concern, jealousy or just nosiness, we overcame all friends' and family advice to "think this through" and bought 200 hectares of rolling land that included a rundown parish called Pievina.

The purported income was from wheat, fava beans, and sheep. The place had a tenant farmer named Franco. With him came a wife, teenage daughter and a handyman whom I suspected was more than passingly interested in the daughter. None of this was my affair. I only hoped by what I'd seen around the place that Franco knew his business. What I knew about my "products" was that sometimes crumbs of them would fall on my wool sweater.

As I turned to my car, I heard Rossini's footsteps coming up behind me.

"Uh, *Signor Dottore*," he started shakily. "There's just one small matter I meant to tell you about your new property. It was such a small thing I simply kept putting it out of my mind."

I've been an investment target long enough to know when bad news is about to be dispensed. I spun around to within inches of Rossini's face and unintentionally spat out, "What ... small matter?"

"Please, no, don't become excited. It is not anything you imagine. In fact, one might even consider a bit of most excellent fortune has come your way." The poor man was sweating profusely and trying to force a smile through a now quivering mouth.

"All right, Rossini," a name I had never used so disrespectfully, "What's the deal? You know I've been around the block and I'm not in the mood for any 'small matter' other than what I've paid for. Get to the point."

"Yes, yes! Of course. Certainly you've seen how well the parish looks. The grass is always cut. The drives are always raked. The olive trees trimmed."

"Yeah! Yeah! Franco and his man do a fine job. I'm most satisfied."

"No, *Signor Dottore*, you don't understand. There is another tenant on the property who does all this work ... for free!"

"Rossini, you've got two minutes to explain yourself."

"*Si, Si, Dottore*. You will see this is a good bit of luck for you."

A certain glint in his puffy black eyes made me want to punch him in the face.

"Yes, back in 1943 during the war, the Germans came here and passed through Pievina. For some reason which no one knows, they shot Paolo's, uh, that's his name, father, mother and fourteen-year-old sister. Paolo, himself only ten, was spared as he was down in a small valley tending the sheep but, of course, when the poor boy came running up he found the horror of his whole family dead. Before anyone else arrived, he had dragged them over behind the parish church and buried them. To anyone's knowledge he has never spoken a word since that day.

"Go on," I said, now knowing the meaning of the three parallel humps between the small church and its perimeter wall.

"Paolo," continued Rossini, "was cared for for a while by the parish priest. When he was eighteen and the farm could no longer support the church, it was deconsecrated and the priest moved away. While Paolo wouldn't leave, for some odd reason he donated the farm, the houses and

173

the church to the local order of monks ..."

"Wait a second. I've got a clean title. I had it checked."

"*Si! Si!* Let me finish. The monks already have a monastery, as you well know, just over there. Thinking the boy was going to join them, they accepted the donation and immediately sold it to the family from whom you bought it. Paolo just never left and the owners were content to let him stay. He is most useful and keeps the house grounds in exceptionally good condition. But, and here a malevolent twinkle escaped Rossini's narrowed eyes, should you ever need the property where he lives ... well, let's just say it would be no problem legally, if you understand my meaning," he said again extending his hand to which I rudely turned my back.

"OK, Rossini. I'll check this out with my lawyers and you'll hear from me if what you say is any problem."

As I opened the door and swung into the seat of my car, I noted with no small satisfaction the deflated look on the previously imperious face of *Signor* Aldo Rossini.

When we drove through the gates into the yard of our new house, the Franco family and the hired man were all standing there waiting, having been forewarned by Rossini. He was trying, in some way I'm sure, to redeem himself in my eyes.

The scene reminded me of one of those old English films where the return of the family is occasion for the full turnout of the large house staff. Well, in this case it wasn't so grand an affair. Hastily called in from the fields, both Franco and his man were still sweaty with their boots caked in mud but, with hats in hand, trying to look dignified. Both *Signora* Franco and the girl were wringing their plump hands in wet aprons having just come from the wash room.

"*Bon giorno*," I started out.

"Excuse me, *Signor* Crane, but to speak Italian is no necessary. The previous owners were of English and we all speak except for Guillermo here," tossing his head towards the hired man with no little disdain. "He's a good worker but not the sharpest fork in the drawer," he said flashing a smile of immaculate teeth.

"Yes, well, we'll see. One of my interests is fluency in Italian," I said in Italian, not without causing a sag in Franco's face. Off to a bad start here, I thought. "Well, *Signor* Franco," I said in English, "please introduce us. We've met your wife, of course."

A brightened Franco took a step up and in almost a strut turned and formally proclaimed, "*Dottore* and Mrs. Crane, it is my honor and pleasure to present to you my wife, Antonia, and my daughter, Brigitte." Both women curtsied. "This is Guillermo, your hired man. We have lived and served this parish property for three generations and are proud to be asked to continue on in your behalf."

I silently breathed a sigh of relief. Apparently I had what I needed not to bring further ruin to the formerly prosperous property which, besides the land, included several outbuildings for the machinery and livestock, the tenant housing, the main house and of all things a small, deconsecrated church. I could only imagine when the parish was much larger before the war that it was typical for each large farm to need to keep the workers close to the work which had to continue seven days a week. My wife's plans for a bed and breakfast called for the little church to be a restaurant.

I knew exactly what I wanted to do first. Assuming the Francos certainly didn't want to stand around passing the time of day with us, I suggested to Phyllis to organize the transfer of the stuff from our car and told everyone we'd meet later.

Without waiting for an answer I took off towards the creek valley behind the church. There was a small olive orchard that hid the creek but I could hear its musical sound just beyond. As I came through a final dense hedge of cedar, I stopped short with an almost audible gasp of amazement. There before me was almost a mind clip from a Walt Disney thought. I can't help describing it any other way.

The gentle stream passed about fifty yards in front of a picturesque slate roof cottage around which were animals of every description and type: goats, sheep, ducks, chickens, a cow, two cats, a dog, song birds, neatly tended gardens and a huge, gnarled shade tree to the side with a well under it. If Snow White had come to the door I would not have been surprised.

After taking it in for a few minutes, I composed myself and called, "Hello! Hello the house!"

Every one of a hundred creatures stopped its pecking, chewing or sleeping and turned towards me. I felt an incredible sensation of intrusion I've never felt before or since.

At first, nothing stirred. Then, from the shadowed doorway, a man appeared. He was older but he stood straight and firm. You could tell immediately from his eyes, the color of his skin, and full head of short-cropped hair he was what one would call healthy. He wore simple clothes of the country but of good quality and condition.

He said not a word to me in greeting or question so I uneasily became aware if there was to be any communication, it would have to come from me.

"My name is Doctor Robert Crane and I have recently purchased the parish. Only this morning did I find out the parish includes this house and land."

He did not answer but continued to look at me.

"I understand you care for the main parish grounds and live here in exchange. I'm not really sure what to say about it because it was not told to me until just this morning, as I said." I felt stupid and was struggling to understand why.

"Look, the place looks great - which is one of the reasons my wife and I bought it - so I guess we'll keep things the way they are except, for one thing. Rossini, the agent who handled the sale, said you're not paid. Well, since I didn't know I bought this property where you live, I don't feel right about accepting your services for free so I'd like to start paying you, if that's all right?"

After a few moments which started to feel uncomfortable, to my utter amazement he nodded, then slowly stepped back into the cottage and closed the door so softly I didn't hear the latch click. I suddenly became aware again that the eyes of all the animals in the yard were on me as if to say, "OK, you may now leave." I did.

"What's wrong with you?" Phyllis asked me after dinner. "Was my pici undercooked?"

"No, it was wonderful. I'm sorry. I can't get something off my mind and it's really bothering me."

"What, my darling?" she said with the real concern that endeared her so to me. She immediately came to sit by my side.

"I know this is all new and nothing is going to go exactly the way we planned but...."

"No, no! You don't understand. I've wanted to do this since we first came here. I love the place and the Francos are the perfect family for us. It's what else I found out about the place just this morning from that weasel Rossini."

I started from the beginning with Rossini's insolence and finished with what had happened just a few hours ago.

At first, Phyllis just wrinkled her brow, like when she was puzzling something out, and then she said, "Well, the place looks great and we do, in fact, control the situation and it's late with nothing to be done about it tonight. I think you were right in the first place. Let's wait and see what happens."

Phyllis always said things in a simple way and one in which logic always prevailed over my more active and devious mind and made me accept things as they were.

"You're right, of course. But I'll never trust that Rossini again. Why do people always ... aw, screw it. Let's go to bed."

Sunrise and cocks crowing caught me in a sound sleep which my years as a doctor taught me to get wherever and whenever I could, however, I was determined to change that as well. My plan was to work hard, eat well, think, read, write, become more in tune with living instead of out of touch with life.

Then I heard it. The scraping of a rake on gravel. I

rolled over to wake Phyllis but she was already up and gone. Some farmer I was!

Within minutes I was dressed and in the now warm kitchen.

"Well, you were right," Phyllis started, "he's one unusual dude. He's been raking, trimming and hauling for over an hour. I went out to introduce myself and he stopped only long enough to doff his hat, bow and then just continued on working. I offered him coffee and I'm not sure he even heard me. I'm not sure, Doc (she always called me that ever since med school). He's pretty weird."

Phyllis baked bread that afternoon and took it to Paolo's house. She came back with the same exclamations of his house, animals and gardens.

"It was incredible!" she almost squealed. "The whole place was like something out of a Kincaide painting. Did the animals just look at you like you were some kind of freak? Did you see the vegetables? Why don't the animals eat his gardens? Who designed the place ... the Seven Dwarfs? I mean ...."

"Stop! I know! I know!"

"I left the bread on the window sill by the door. I hope the dogs don't eat it ... somehow I don't think they will," she mused looking distant for a moment.

"I don't think so, either."

The next morning, rising earlier, I almost tripped over a basket by the door brimming with vegetables, wine, eggs ... more of the best food I've ever seen.

That's pretty much how it went for the next several weeks. Any small kindness was returned several fold. Until the day the local priest arrived, I felt things were about as good as they could get.

His black Peugeot crunched into the drive at a pre-determined time he had mysteriously called to arrange, not telling us why. As he came to a stop, he could hardly get out fast enough to come over and pump my hand.

"*Signor! Signor! Signor!* Such a pleasure. Such an honor. We are so blessed to have people ... esteemed people such as yourselves come into our little community. Such generosity! Such selflessness!"

"Whoa! Whoa! Father! What in Go... in the heck are you talking about?"

Confusedly, the simple country priest looked left then right and said simply, "The money!"

"What money?"

"The money you send every week. It has meant more than you can know. Food for the orphans, paint for the church. Oh! It's not vast but with your support has come other support and that has meant new interest in the church and what it stands for. Simply, my church is standing room only and it's all due to you and what you've done!"

The poor priest almost looked sick with uncertainty as my face must have reflected total befuddlement.

"*Escuse, Signor*, but every week for three months our parish has received a significant amount of money in cash that would pay a full-time person of some importance. The postmark is of this parish and I only assumed it was from you. Forgive me if I have gone too far but we are very poor and such benefit to us is unknown. I felt it only proper to thank you."

It suddenly dawned on me what the priest was saying.

While we had not actually discussed how much I was to pay Paolo, I took it on myself to pay him more than a fair wage because, quite frankly, he did more than one would expect of two people. He worked ten to fourteen hours a day. The only time he took off was Sunday for market day when he sold his privately produced vegetables, fruits and eggs. It now became clear that the money I left for Paolo was being sent to this parish priest.

That was it for me. After unsuccessfully trying to explain things to the priest, he left still thinking us his benefactor. I sent for Franco.

It was just past the lunch hour so Franco came quickly, still a little groggy from his mid-day nap.

"*Signor*, Brigitte has said you wish to see me. Is everything all right?"

"Yes and no. Tell me everything you know about this Paolo."

With this Franco drew himself up and took a deep breath

"His is a story of great sadness and yet soaring triumph. Perhaps he is what saints are truly supposed to be. I have told all of this to no one out of respect for his own wishes but feel you are a man who should know. Someone should know before it is too late, meaning, of course, that he is now over seventy years old.

"To begin, you know the tragedy of his youth. Imagine hearing shots in the peace of this place and to return to find your entire dear family shot dead for a reason no one will ever know. How can one say that something so horrid is the will of a benevolent God? Signor, I ask you that.

"In any event, this small boy of ten years digs their

181

graves beside the church and buries them – alone. At this time all the men were gone to war and the women lived in town.

"He lived here alone for three years during the war until the parish was reopened by an uncle and the boy was taken in and cared for by the parish priest. Sadly, the farm failed and was deserted which resulted in the deconsecration of the church.

"The boy was now of age and, for reasons of his own, deeded the parish property to the monastery just north of here. The monks had no use for the property and sold it. The boy built the cottage and has lived there ever since."

"How does he live? He gives what I pay him to the church?"

A wry smile crossed Franco's lips. "Go to the market Sunday. Go early. His vegetables, eggs and cheese are the most sought after in Tuscany. He would anger the other farmers except he only produces what he needs to live on. He has a gift and could be a rich man if he wanted. Actually, he may be the richest man I know," Franco mused.

"You mentioned some very strong descriptions of his purpose and saintly character. So far I see little of it in your story," I interjected.

"*Si*. This is the part that makes you wonder about God and his ways. You see, Paolo probably saved several hundred lives by staying here! As you know, the war brought out the absolute worst in us as humans. I am ashamed of my own small role in accepting the fascist way and the ensuing persecution and murder of so many innocents.

182

"First, they came as single families - Jews escaping the Venetian ghetto, gypsies, homosexuals, writers. In fact, the safe haven of the parish in Pievina became one of the great secrets of the Italian underground.

"Remember all of it was being run by an adolescent boy of eleven to thirteen years who never spoke. He grew the food, stole clothing, drew maps and generally passed God-only-knows-how-many people through the basement of that small church. God's plan? Harsh? I am not smart enough to say but I must believe it so."

"Wait a minute," I interrupted. "How could all this happen and no one has ever heard of it before?"

"Signor, the whole thing began and ended in total secrecy. The people who came here had to swear on all they held sacred to never tell another unless they themselves needed the place ... a pledge that was to survive for their lives and until this day it has been kept. You see, I was one of those who was sheltered here after I saw the evil of the fascists. I break my pledge, but in honor of this great man, not in disrespect."

After Franco's departure, I sat by the wall of the parish enclosure that overlooked the valley now verdant in spring greenery. I felt his presence before I heard the soft crunch of the gravel beneath Paolo's boots, but I did not turn to face him.

His gentle voice should have startled me because I didn't expect it, but somehow it didn't.

"He has told you?"

"Yes and I will honor the pledge if you wish but I want you to know I will never leave this place."

"Do as you will for I too will never leave." This was to

183

be the one and only time we ever spoke.

The next morning there was an eerie silence about the place and I intuitively knew why. Taking Phyllis without explanation to the cottage, we found his body in bed as if he were still sleeping.

Within hours there was a fresh grave alongside the three long-since-forgotten graves of so many years ago.

Within days the hundreds of mourners arrived both singly and in groups. They left without comment, flowers or permission.

Of course, it drew the attention of the local Carabinieri captain who arrived and wanted to know what was going on ... what was the fresh looking grave all about ... and why wasn't he notified? An official investigation would have to take place.

When I asked when that might be, however, he noted that they were very busy at the moment and it might take some time, in fact years, to get to this matter of so little importance. He looked at me for a moment and his eyes told me all I needed to know.

Guillermo (who turned out to be a lot sharper "fork" than papa thought) and Brigitte married and I gave them the cottage as a wedding present. Most of the animals still populate the place and under Guillermo's hand the gardens are as fruitful as ever, especially with the two children there to help.

As for me and Phyllis, we never did the B & B but instead tried to live the rest of our days in honor of a good man.

AMERICAN
MADONNA

"**A**lright, ladies and gentlemen," the auctioneer announced with no small amount of ceremony. "The moment has arrived for the last item to be sold tonight and, let's be honest," condescending, all-knowing smile, "this is the main reason we're here tonight. The so-called American Madonna, the last work of Howard Ames and the only one of his works still held privately outside the world's greatest museums. Completed in 1933 at the height of the Great Depression, its multiple themes of beauty, love and hope became an immediate inspiration for a nation of hopeless millions when it surfaced in 1938. Ames was found dead in front of the completed canvas and the mythological legend of the unnamed painting was begun. Owned by kings, dictators and billionaires it has never found a comfortable or lasting place of repose. It's subject matter engendered the name for which it became known and, like the Mona Lisa, part of the allure is the mysterious subject of the work which will probably never be known. Perhaps tonight this greatest of American works will find its true and final home. The bidding will start at ten million dollars. Thank you sir. Do I have fifteen?"

Howard Ames was cold. As he lay shivering in bed, the thought crossed his mind that he was always either cold or hungry since he usually had to make a choice between coal, food or paint, and paint always won out. Whether Ames was cold or hungry, or both, it mattered little to him. It was for the act of creating he lived.

He had long since stopped thinking that, like Van Gogh, he had never in his life sold a painting. Oh, he had traded a few to bars for a plate of food only to see the work hung in the dark hall leading to the toilets and he had drawn sketches from a cardboard sign advertising, "Your likeness in less than 10 minutes," for a drink but these accommodations could hardly be counted as a sale. There was a depression on and the last thing people wanted or could afford for that matter, was art.

All this was, of course, lost on Ames himself, for the need to create didn't necessarily burn in his breast like an art history book ideal but rather was for him a necessity of life not unlike breathing. If anyone asked, which they rarely did, his answer was always the same simple, "I paint, therefore I am," to which most people responded with a queer look and a slugging down of whatever they were drinking and a quick move away from the strange paint splattered man standing before them with eyes that looked in your direction but didn't seem to actually see you.

Ames had always drawn. His mother putting pencil and paper in front of him was his first memory. Married to a prosperous but loutish farmer, his mother longed for the more refined life and thus encouraged her son in his art which his father never missed an opportunity to dismiss as "sissy stuff", not even giving his son's efforts scant recognition by calling it "work".

At sixteen, Ames was beaten almost to death by his

father who came in from the fields to find his wife posing nude for the boy. Ames left for good the next morning. His mother sent him twenty dollars a month until she died. Ames would never have known she had passed except for the fact that one month the money stopped coming. Then just as oddly to Ames who only noticed the interruption as a nuisance to being able to buy paints, the money resumed coming once more.

This morning started like every other with Ames rolling out of bed in the attic closet of a room afforded him for some unknown reason by the madam of the whorehouse downstairs. The "whore with a heart of gold" Ames supposed but never dwelt on such things. He gave her a painting every week or so which she always accepted with a mysterious smile and a genuine note of appreciation in which Ames found a small measure of pleasant affirmation. As long as he entered and left by the fire escape the madam was content to let the strange man pretty much alone. She did require him to bathe each Sunday morning when the house was closed. The girls teased him mercilessly but it was strictly against the rules of the house to give "it" away so that was the end of it since Ames never had any money.

There was, however, one of the girls that interested Ames which is how it was with him. Something about a coal vendor, and old woman sleeping in a doorway, a child begging in the street that created an inspiration in him that he could not resist. Nor did he try. His paintings captured the essence of a feeling, a moment that seemed to satisfy some deep requirement of his soul.

On rare occasions when the end result disappointed

him he would rip the canvas to shreds using dirty fingers, palette knife and teeth until his face was smeared beyond recognition and the offending piece lay in a pile before his heaving, sweating, drained hulk. He would cry for days and lock himself in his room without food or drink, only to emerge ragged and spent but with a look of indomitable determination in his eyes that was so fierce it scared even the madam. He would then paint the same subject again.

The woman of his interest was the most popular resident of the house. He had never spoken a word to her even though he suffered the worst at her sharp tongued taunts that wounded him both as a man and an artist.

"His dick is probably as useless as he is."

"He has so much paint on his clothes he should sell himself."

"It's good he never sells anything he might come snooping around for a place to spend the money."

All the while he would lock his eyes to hers and with no words between them she would have to turn away either with a derisive laugh or a dismissive wave of her elegant hand.

Ames' tortured sleepless nights were only broken once in a great while when he would dream of the woman. Dreams of her perfect body, her shining raven hair, her white alabaster skin like the Cupid at the entrance of the house and her eyes. Oh, her eyes! Her almost translucent blue eyes had given her the trade moniker of "Sky". He wanted what he would never have. He loved her.

After an unusually long period of not seeing the woman, Ames was startled when the madam opened the door as he was exiting the tub where he was performing the rule of his tenancy. He instinctively grabbed a towel to obscure his privates which caused the madam to throw back her head in raucous laughter.

"Darlin', you've got nothing I haven't seen and nothing I want. I come to tell you about Sky."

"Sky?" he repeated dumbly.

"Look, sweetheart, I make my living watching people and I know you love that one. She is a beauty and she's done well for me even though she's cost me plenty these past few months. I thought you'd like to know she had her baby."

"Her baby?"

"Oh, you poor thing. Yes, she got careless and got knocked up. It happens. Hazard of the profession. Anyway, it's a beautiful girl and Sky is okay. Don't know what we'll do with the child though."

Without another word the madam turned and left Ames standing alone in the room in a puddle of water, still clutching the towel in a clumsy attempt to cover himself. Ames had already exited and entered another part of his thoughts. He stared at nothing for some moments then dropped the towel, dressed while still wet and hurried to his room. There he collected canvass, easel, brushes and selected the best of his paints.

As he passed through the door into the hall he knew he was risking his only refuge but it didn't matter. He knew he was breaking the rule but he had to go. He knew the woman would laugh at him but he didn't care.

His soft, hesitant knock on the door was answered by, "Yeah, who is it?"

"It's me, the painter from the attic. I heard you had a

baby. May I come in?"

"Sure, honey," she laughed, "why not? Everybody else has."

Ames gently pushed open the door, entered and softly closed it behind him.

There, propped up in bed, was the woman. Her shining black hair fell to one side over her shoulder and covering her breast. At the other breast she held the child who was greedily sucking its meal.

"What do you want, Mr. Walking Painting from the attic?" she mocked. "And who said you could close the door? You wanna get me fired?"

"No. She's beautiful," Ames choked out as best as he could.

"Yeah, well, it's not exactly what I had in mind."

"So, you've seen it. So what?"

"I want to paint you."

The woman's laugh startled the feeding child and it started to whimper until she put the nipple back to its mouth.

"Well, I ain't going anywhere so go ahead but you got to pay me."

"I don't have any money."

"Yeah, that's what I figured. Tell you what. I'll take the painting just like Madam does ... deal?"

"Okay. Sure," said Ames as he moved quickly to set his easel at the chosen angle to capture what he was feeling. What he knew that the woman didn't was that he had to do this and it was not for money.

Ames never painted faster in his life. The moment had to be captured just as it was. Blessedly, the child fell asleep in the cradling arms of the woman who, for some unknown reason, even to herself, remained still and stared directly at Ames. He could already feel the chill and the fever beginning to rage inside his still wet clothes.

Her look was an expressionless blank of simplicity that Ames interpreted with every fiber of his being and every bit of his skill. More than ever before with any other of his countless subjects, his mind transcended his body to another world where only artists are admitted. His life was his vision. His vision his dream. His dream his life.

"You don't look so good. Are you done?" The words came from somewhere Ames could hear and startled him back to the place and time of the woman's room and the fact that he was shaking uncontrollably.

"Yes."

"Lemme see it."

"No."

"Whaddya mean, no. It's mine ain't it?"

"Yes, I'm going to take it to my room and fill in the background."

"Yeah, sure. You're gonna take it upstairs and jerk off. I'm gonna send Madam up in the morning and if you don't give it to her I'll get you thrown out of here. You got that old man?"

Stung almost to tears, Ames could only mumble, "Yes," as he gathered his things. At the door, he turned and locked his eyes to the woman's as he had so many times before and said simply, "I love you."

"Get out!"

Ames could hear her almost hysterical laughter mingled with a child's cry as he made his way back to his room.

The next morning the woman awoke to find the madam standing beside her bed.

"Wha ... whatsa matter?" was all the woman could manage as she struggled to awaken.

"Look," choked the older woman as she turned the canvass for the other to look at.

"Uh, oh. It's beautiful! Is that really me?" she said in spite of herself.

"Oh yes. It really is and I don't know if I've ever seen anything quite as beautiful in my life".

"It's mine you know," said the woman with a wary look at the madam.

"Yes, I know and you shall have it the day you leave this place."

"Whaddya mean? What did that crazy old bastard tell you?"

"Nothing. He's dead and I'm closing the house."

The woman did leave. She took the child and the painting and was never heard from again. The farthest back the painting's ownership could be traced was to a pawn shop in Abilene where it was left for $25 and never redeemed.

When the auctioneer's hammer fell the painting was sold for a record price. The old woman who had bid anonymously by phone and won smiled to herself for after having owned so many of Ames' works, she now had the one she most desired.

❄   ❄   ❄

Thank you for reading.
Please review this book. Reviews help others find
Absolutely Amazing eBooks and inspire us to keep
providing these marvelous tales.

If you would like to be put on our email list to receive
updates on new releases, contests, and promotions, please
go to AbsolutelyAmazingEbooks.com and sign up.

ABOUT THE AUTHORS

F.W. Belland and Chris Belland are brothers born in Miami, Florida, in 1944 and 1948 respectively.

The brothers grew up in Miami when it was much different from the Miami of today. There was a distinctive rural influence. The home in which they lived was on the edge of what was the Everglades but is now a developed part of West Kendall. Some of the neighbors around them were early pioneers of Miami. Their closest friends were the founders of Lemon City which eventually became the City of Miami. The family patriarch, Captain Bob Douthit, was one of the storied barefoot mailmen.

After high school, the brothers took divergent paths. Fred served in the Marine Corps in Vietnam and eventually graduated from Florida State University. Chris went to the University of Pennsylvania, Wharton School of Finance and Commerce, and moved back to Miami.

In 1973, both brothers moved to the island city of Key West, Florida, where they were instrumental in restoring the center of the historic downtown area on Duval Street, which is today a vibrant tourist destination.

The stories contained here resonate from the rich history of early Florida and its close contacts with Central and South America.

Today, Chris still lives in Key West with his wife, Piper. Fred makes his home on the rim of a volcanic lake in Nicaragua, with his wife, Carmen and their two children. The third printing of his novel, The True Sea, (Holt, Rinehart and Winston, N.Y.) came out last year. He is also the author of the novel, Fleshwound (Jove Paperback, N.Y.).

The New
Atlantian Library

NewAtlantianLibrary.com

or AbsolutelyAmazingEbooks.com

or AA-eBooks.com